C000303032

REDEMPTION

REDEMPTION

J.I. MCKINNEY

ISBN: 978-1-64871-672-0   (Paperback Edition)
ISBN: 978-1-64871-673-7   (Hardcover Edition)
ISBN: 978-1-64871-670-6   (E-book Edition)

Some characters and events in this book are fictitious. Any similarity to real persons, living or dead, is coincidental and not intended by the author.

Book Ordering Information

Phone Number: 347-901-4929 or 347-901-4920
Email: info@globalsummithouse.com
Global Summit House
www.globalsummithouse.com

Printed in the United States of America

Contents

ALINA WAS SITTING on the patio enjoying the smell of the roses beside her. She discovered them in a meadow not far from where her house was and named them 'Captain's Rose'. She was regreting her decision but knew that it was the correct one. The attacks were becoming more frequent and their severity was increasing exponentially. To save her ship and her crew faking her death was necessary. She had asked Danielle keep her plan a secret even from Captain Davis. Alina knew obeying her was a conflict of interest because Mike was now her Captain. The head stone she designed intentionally contained an error on it. Only those who knew her middle name would have seen it. Alina had all she needed right here. Power from a small cold fusion reactor, the plumbing designed by her structural engineers and her food supply was guaranteed because Danielle would send food to her every six days. If she felt she needed or wanted to contact a ship of the Planetary Council there was a communications station inside. If a ship was near her a warning system activated and she could cloak everything if necessary. She desperately missed her ship and crew. Cerollon's would send up regular patrols and fly far and wide to scan for any one or thing that might be a threat to her.

After hurting them the way she did it was unlikely her crew would accept her back. So here she was on World One Sam all by herself. That wasn't quite true some of her crew volunteered to stay and watch over her house when she was aboard the Long Island. There was a small town across the lake that was growing all the time. Most of those who stayed behind brought their families with them. She would hear their children playing in the distance and it was a pleasing sound to her. It was forbidden for the children to go the Captain's house. There were things there that was extremely dangerous and no place for playing. As she was reflecting on her crew and how she wished she was still with them her alert system went off. Going into her house she looked at the monitor screen to see what ships were approaching. The ship identifications came up and they were the Tarnet Command Ship and the New Iberia. When she saw they were approaching at battle speed she thought that can't be good. Standing by the comm system she was listening to transmissions between the ships. They were looking for her. Time to step up and face the music.

Confession Time

S HE TOLD HER Tretret team with her that there would be company coming probably hostile. She meant it jokingly but her team did not take it that way and prepared to resist those that would be transporting down. The Captain was their responsibility and they would not fail to protect her. On hearing that someone was approaching and might be hostile six Cerollon took to the sky and was ready to attack from the air if needed. Strefdan and Tretrets formed a wall encircling the Captain. Lomgren with her were prepared to attack and destroy any threat to her. When Captain Davis, the Tarnet Commander, her Tretret Commander on the ship and Danielle materialized her team was confused about the hostiles part. The Tretret commander went up to her looked into her eyes and confirmed that she was indeed his Captain. He asked her forgiveness for not being more attentive to her well being and safety. She took his face in her hands and softly said she had to do what she did because too many of her family were dying because of her. Still not sure what was going on some of her team stood between them and the Captain. Alina called the Cerollon's down things were ok. Captain Davis started to chew her out when a Strefdan blade was placed against his neck and was warned to speak to her with respect.

Realizing that they were only showing their devotion to her he softened his tone. Alina invited all four to sit and she would talk first. First off Danielle knew from the beginning of her plan. Alina had explained her idea in exacting detail as well as to why she felt it was absolutely necessary. Then ordered her not to speak to anyone of it. Now that Mike was her Captain it was a conflict of trust between them and she apologized for putting her in that position. Danielle interjected that had the Captain asked her about it she would be obligated by the rules of command to tell him everything. He did not ask about it so she did not mention it. Captain Davis was going to respond but then understood that Danielle did not refuse to tell him. Like she said he had not inquired. A point to keep in mind next time. Alina continued about the numerous attacks against her, their severity and realized as long as she was alive the attacks would continue. What concerned her more was her family, her crew. They were being killed because of her. Hence the neccessity of her death.

Alina did not know her hunters. All she knew was members of her crew were dying to protect her and it had to stop. She turned to Mike and said "Did you see all those graves there? Why do you think there are so many? They died for me. I had to find a way to save my crew. I couldn't tell you or any one in the Planetary Council because it had to look real. My hunters had to believe my death was real." With obvious sorrow she said that she could not return to the ship because her crew would not forgive her for the pain she caused them. So she exiled herself here to protect them. Danielle spoke up and said "Captain I sent a patrol to the lunar city cemetery to check on your grave and the headstone has been destroyed, your casket cut open, the body dismembered and the head is missing." Alina's eyes were filing with tears as she realized she was still being hunted. Her crew was still in jeopardy. She sat back heavily and was looking at Mike and the Tarnet commander across from her. Almost inaudibly she asked now what did she do?

The Tarnet commander said what you do is return to your ship and resume your rightful place as Captain. If you are being hunted what better place to be than aboard a ship with massive fire power at your command. Captain Davis agreed and when they transported aboard the Long Island he would transfer command back to her. Besides commanding two ships was a cutting in on his beauty sleep. Alina was going to say it didn't help but said nothing. Her crew would learn she was placing them first in trying to protect her crew and defended them the only way she knew how. Apologies were still necessary. She would gather the entire crew and try to explain why she had to hurt them. She did want not any more to die because of her. Alina knew once she resumed command there was a very strong possibility the attacks would begin again. Her Tretret commander promised that he and his team would be more vigilant to all around her and question anything that didn't fit. As for as her hunters they would discover that sometimes the prey becomes the hunter. William decided in order to protect the Captain better the prisoners in section four would have to be sent off the ship in case one of them was a mole for her hunters. They would have to be transported off before the Captain returned aboard. He did not consider their being days from the nearest planet a problem. Section four was empty by the time Alina arrived on the ship.

Celebration

WHEN THE CREW learned Alina was alive and wanted to see the crew in the common area, as many as would fit, the remainder would hear her on the ship's internal monitor's there were cheers from every quarter of the ship. Alina's remarks took about forty minites with an apology that she regretted hurting them as she did but it was necessary to protect them. It was Alina who wanted the entire crew to witness the change of command back to her. The celebration dinner was an event Alina would never forget. She had been thinking that since she had been on World One she felt younger and healthier. Her reactions were more like they were when she was much younger. Her mental sharpness higher and alertness increased. Probably her imagination. Since resuming command she had to look over the ship again. Her Tretrets always near her, always looking around and the Lomgren with her listening and smelling the air for anything not there before. The Strefdan blades gleamed and their blades sharp enough to cut deeply with the gentlest touch. Occasionally she would put her arm on one of the Amdor's she knew from before and talked with them like family, which as far as Alina was concerned they were. Yes they were her crew and there had to be a line between crew and Captain. Normally the Cerollons did not fly in the ships hallways but William changed that. If the Captain was not on the bridge or her quarters there would be several above her at all times,

Explanations to the Planetary Council took more finesse. After hearing of her graves desecration the council agreed there was an unknown enemy and while it seemed to center around her they were now the council's enemy as well. The Tarnet commander briefed his ships on the situation surrounding the Captain of the Long Island and the possibility that attacks could be taken against them as well. Increased alert status was ordered for all Planetary Council ships. A decision that Alina was having difficulty making was about Prime Minister Brown. Does she tell him or let it rest with him believing her dead? Briefings were longer because of her absence. So much happening about her she was unaware of. Because of the desecrartion of her grave the body's remains were reburied in a different location. Why her hunters wanted the head she could not surmise. Her time on World One Sam had rejuvenated her and she felt ready to continue in her duties. Knowing that there were Cerollon's above her all the time off the bridge she actually felt comforting and more at ease when she moved through the ship. A life form she had not seen before on the ship tried to rush toward her and a Tretret's fist stopped it cold. None aboard had ever seen this life form before either and now it was necessary to determine how it, or they, got aboard and close that breach.

Wiliam seized it and removed it to section four immediately. Danielle and William would use a Medusan to get the answers they needed. One of the Lomgren with her told her that they would remember it's smell and lock on to it any time it was near long before any threat was possible. She thanked them and told her commander she wanted as much information on the life form as possible. Contact medical bay and have complete physiological scans done and recorded. Find out what it was and where it came from. The Medusan would get the most vital information from it. It was well into the evening after dinner that the Captain began to get a picture of just what they had. The life form came aboard in a cargo ship and was trying to get to the Captain because their planet needed assistance. When she was talking to it the Tarnet Commander was standing next to her listening. He had not seen this life form before and there was no record of it in Planetary Council records. The Volitny ship would take it aboard and transport it to the council's headquarters and it would be dealt with there. William set down rules that all cargo ships coming aboard be scanned first kilometers away from the ship before being allowed closer. Once cleared they could be brought in to the landing bay.

The Medusan was able to get from the life form there were four of them aboard. A condition three surrounding the Captain and Danielle was immediately enforced. All crew members were set to look for anything that looked suspicious and advise William. One hour into the search two were found in the food stores area trying to gather as much as they could carry. Another was in the weapons control trying to disable the weapons to allow their escape. The fourth was still awaiting it's trip to the council. The two in the food stores would join their friend in the journey. The one in the weapons control was found by a Lomgren who wasted no time killing it. William sent it into the coldness of space. Engineers and Sinefors began an exhausting diagnosis of the weapons system checking every aspect where they discovered tampering.

When William and her Tretret commander were satisfied there was no further threat to the Captain or the ship the alert was cancelled. Alina had a copy of the incident report sent to the New Iberia. The Tarnet Commander still with her would return to his ship now that the Captain was safe. The bond the two shared was an unbreakable friendship. As Alina had said before she had his back and he had hers. The question William had was were these four the moles they were seeking? After many hours of debating with herself the pros and cons of contacting the Prime Minister again she decided she would through a contact already in London. It would not be an easy task explaining things and she preferred someone else do it more diplomatically. Staerr told her an ncoming message on normal channels from the New iberia. She said, "Staerr Connect message please." "Captain how are you doing?" "Never mind me what is going on Alina? Another attempt on you already?"

"The one that tried to get to me was stopped in his tracks by my team. The other three were stopped before any real damage to the ship could be done. All three survivng are on the way to the council as we speak. You will be happy to know the Tarnet commander stayed with me throughout the event never leaving my side. There was no possibility of my being harmed." Captain Davis," the Tarnet was saying," I was with the Captain when the life form was being questioned. It seemed more apparent they needed food and was willing to steal it and disable any systems preventing their escape. The engineers and Sinefors found several systems comprimised and are working on restoring full capability." Captain Davis shook his head when he read the report. Some one was targeting Alina. Because she was a female and felt she was weaker? What ever the reason the truth was there. If they had not found out already she was not an easy target to eliminate.If there was any doubt Captain Davis's ship would make that task even more complicated to achieve.

William had been in contact with Michael updating him on everything including all he learned about the three captured on the Long Island. When this thing touched the New Iberia, and he did not doubt it would, Michael's position would be stronger when it did. Knowing his enemy beforehand gave him an advantage before trouble found them. Transmissions between the Long island and a relay station was puzzling to Davis. Alina seemed to understand just fine. Edinburgh was solid. ESA was on the cusp of major event. English room has been in contact, no trouble. Send first try. The British Prime Minister answered there was no problem he understood her decision, reply at first opportunity. Edinburgh medical program breaking ground in medicine everyday and the ESA was on the edge of a major space discovery of their own. The Long Island was exploring an unknown area of space and long range scannners were operating at maximum capacity. Staerr said, "Captain we have something at extreme range bearing one three zero degrees at six million kilometers. This is measuring at approximately fifteen hundred kilometers across and six hundred kilometers long. We are not reading any power signatures or life signs."

Riding The Constellation

ALINA SAID, "STAERR send to New Iberia and all council ships in the region. Advise the discovery's nature and request the council send teams to our position soonest." Turning she called Danielle, her commander and William beside her, "The only reason for a ship that size is if those piloting it are moving their entire civilization. Why would a civilization be moving at one time? Maintain distance from ship. Until we know more set condition three, advise other ships of condition three alert, prepare three battle craft for immediate deployment and target the ship. Weapons at my command. I want the most complete scan of the vessel we can do." "Danielle said, "The New Iberia is about three ship periods from us and the rest are within eight periods. The council advises they will send teams to the ship. Are there any discernible markings as to what it is called?" Alina thought for a moment and said "Tell them it is the Constellation." "Constellation, sending now Captain. Ship is at condition three, other ships advised and weapons at your command." She was talking to Danielle and wanted to consult Captain Davis on procedure from here on secure channel.

Mike said, "Have you ever given thought to a quiet day Alina? As to the Constellation I agree. Who ever sent it was or is moving their entire civilization at one time. I recommend you send probes and test the air for microscopic forms or toxic fumes in the air. Several of our ships will do a complete scan of the exterior primarily and if probes detect no problems internally then we will send research teams to finish investigation. A ship that size will take months if not years to analyze. Probably have to tow it to the council until we can figure out the propulsion and piloting procedures. In the mean time think your decision for condition three is a wise one. Maintain your distance from the ship until more ships arrive and we can plan on what we are going to do in detail." For some reason there was a foreboding feeling when she looked at the ship.

Leaning over to talk with Danielle confidentially she told her something about this was not right. If scans pick up any life forms at all pull all ships back and standby for attack commands. Danielle moved to the combat command control sections verifying all systems were at readiness. Both had decided that targeting the bridge and propulsion engines was the best option with out destroying the entire ship and quite possibly all alive on the ship. Alina was back to having to decide or not decide on genocide of a life form. Forward weapons were set for maximum power. At this setting a planet would be turned to dust. A ship this size, as large as it is, would be completely obliterated and unfortunately all aboard as well. Ordering the ship pulled back an additional one hundred kilometers and position raised four hundred kilometers above the ship the Long Island lay in wait for the other ships to arrive. Captain Davis saw that Alina was at a prime attack angle to the Constellation. That meant she felt something was not as it should be with the ship. He sent to all ships coming in recommending full battle stations as a precaution and slow approach speeds. Staerr and Tanya were in constant communicaton on their secure channel. No hint of any thing out of the ordinary would be overlooked no matter how small.

Staerr was telling her that all council ships were slowing approach and taking up different attack positions above and behind the Constellation. Captain Davis was lead incident commander. The bridge of the New Iberia was a cacophony of noise and activity. Additional Tretrets and Strefden were on the bridge to protect the Captain and Danella. Alina commanded "Staerr open hailing to all ships. Captain Davis is lead command ship. Request confirmation of message." As Staerr was confirming message so was Tanya to Captain Davis. Alina hit her comm button engineering replied almost at once. "Captain we are getting mixed signals from probes." Alina was thinking the probes are being jammed. Someone on the ship is trying to conceal their presence and intent. Her thoughts were seconded by the Tarnet Commander. The Volitny ship agreed and moved his ship to a different covering position. The virus carriers came to mind first and the Long Island redirected some of her main weapons to what was surmised to be weapon command centers near the outboard and central sections. A single misstep on the Constellation's part would result in it's annihilation.

The continued confused signals from the probes could be from the material of the Constellation's hull or it could be electronically intentional. Alina had no intention of letting her guard down for a moment. She instructed Danielle to recheck all systems. Speaking to her Tretret commander at her side she was commenting on her bad feelings about this ship. Just something about it was not right and that feeling would not diminish. The doctor called her on the comm and said the probes thus far had not picked up any trace of a virus or anything out of the ordinary. She asked what the atmosphere was like in the ship being detected right now. The answer was there was no atmosphere in the ship. Staerr advised the other council ships of the current probe information. Alina was in closed channel communications with the other Captains and was as baffled how a ship this size could travel across the emptiness of space with no breathable atmosphere. The decision that Mike had to make would affect the council's decision of whether to tow and research or let it go drifting through space. None of the probes signals had indicated any signs of life from any part of the ship. The power signatures were minmal at best. The council engineers would be studying this vessel for a very long time. After a long discussion with the council on closed channels it was decided to go ahead and tow the Constellation to headquarters for examination.

Several engineers would meet the New Iberia and it's towing ships enroute and take the Constellation under their command. Alina at Davis's command broke off her watch and had the Long Island stand down form alert. Turning to the helm officers she said, "Come to three one zero, axis A and set speeds to two thirds ahead." Danielle repeated her command and made sure the correct speed and course was enabled. It took a long time for the Constellation to disappear from view considering its size. About halfway to the council the engineers arrived and boarded the ship. Even with a team of engineers that numbered over two thousand they were seprated by great distances on the ship. The Captain appointed for the Constellation was a Tarnet officer with many years of experience. With that said he was not prepared for command of such a large ship. The Long Island, as large as it is, was dwarfed by the Constellation. The deceased crew members were still at their stations. They would present a problem. The council had no idea who built the ship or where it came from. The technology held many secrets to be yet uncovered. The honor ceremony created by Captain Grant would be used to give the dead final honors. They would not be taken back to the lunar city for burial. That had been reserved by the Captain for her crew that had passed away. World One Sam as a burial site was absolutely out of the question. World One was the Captain's by discovery.

Her burial was staged to protect her and her grave's desecration was a sore point for the council. The dismemberment and the theft of the head was a real concern. Even in death her enemies were still hunting her. The only thing that they had going for them was there was a three percent difference between Strefdan and human DNA. Close enough in DNA structure yet still far enough apart to be different. Without a human for comparison they could not know the head belonged to a Strefdan woman. World Two Terra was off limits by order of the council and World Three Atlantis was proving a huge success. Discoveries made every day was changing the face of history. Proof of civilizations that existed before the planet was buried beneath the waves was bringing theories of just where they truly originated. Some of the artifacts strangely enough showed similarities to some on earth dating from about the year eleven hundred to mid twelve hundred BC. Because of their condition they had to be kept in a saltwater container to protect them. Earth's archeologists would be trying to figure that one out for many years. Similar artifacts on earth when showed to the advisors caused just as much bewilderment. Staerr brought Alina a note folded in half and stood with her back to her as she read. The Prime minister was in Edinburgh at the medical center that was a bustling noisy place since the conference. His security team forced it's way through the crowd to howls of outrage from every direction. A particularly nasty tempered nurse tried to chew them out and faced a pistol inches from her forehead before her next breath. Holding up her hands she backed off. The advisors welcomed the Prime Minister to the center and were briefing him on the advancements that had been coming on a daily basis. These advancemnts were aincent history to the advisors but marvels of science to the staff. Many of the physicians were building their professional reputations on the discoveries the advisors brought to them. Discoveries they did nothing to earn themselves. They simply rode on the backs of the nurses and techs that did the real work and published under their names. Regretfully it was becoming a commonplace event. The real workers were sidestepped so a nameless physician could become a medical authority.

The message was that if she wanted to return to England she would be very welcome. The Centaurs seemed to become a favorite overnight. Pictures and videos of them were everywhere and on the net. Many were thinking if there are Centaurs perhaps out there in space other creatures of Greek mythology also existed. Speculation ran wild about maybe there were Minotaurs or beings with great powers over the sky and weather. The advisors are the most popular people on the earth. Because of Constitutional law in the United States they could not run for governmental posts. Many politicians here were counting their blessings for that. The note also said that other governments were trying to get the advisors to come to their countries and see if they could help them with the overwhelming hunger and drought plagues. Edinburgh physicians, with the aid of the advisors, were making gigantic strides against diseases that seemed unsolvable until now. In Tampa, Florida a science academy of sorts was burning the midnight oil around the clock. Advances with the advisors help were finding solutions to puzzles that physicists and chemical engineers thought impossible in their lifetimes. Nothing seemed unsolvable with their assistance. A hospital in Spirit Lake, Iowa with the advisors guiding them, had grown the first healthy kidney in forty one hours. The kidney was genetically specific for a ten year old girl suffering from renal disease.

Sanwich, England was enjoying the new influx of tourists in their town. Businesses in the area were growing in the financial downfall of popularity of the region. Cryptozoologists were at a loss to explain the life forms that were on display in Sanwich. There was no precedence of any such creatures prior to then. Naysayers were trying to keep further exploration of space from continuing when in their presence was the very reason exploration shoud continue. Exploration was dangerous and should be stopped. The dangers of exploration was a major draw to those who clamored to be in those missions. The promise of marvelous new life forms to interact with held many of those explores in it's grasp. There was a very personal notation to Alina that brought tears to her and a desire to return to England as soon as she could. She said, "Danielle do we have any missions in this sector?" "No Captain. We are clear to navigate at any time." "Set course for the lunar city. Advise Captain Davis of our destination and advise when we are within five periods of lunar orbit. Let Houston and London know of our arrival time. Send a special message to SETI. I am sure they would apreciate that."

"Captain I do not know what this SETI is. What is their mission? I assume they have a specific task." Alina said, "SETI stands for Search for Extra Terrestrial Intelligence. They look for radio signals from intelligent life forms from new worlds. There are several very large array dishes in the New Mexico desert that search the sky endlessly for the signals I mentioned." A bridge officer said, "Like transmissions from us." Staerr said to him, "Exactly like our transmissions. Now that they know there are other intelligent lifeforms in the sky above them their mission is even more imperative to locate them." Alina left the bridge to go to her quartes leaving Danielle in command. As they approached the lunar city she could not help but wonder who her enemy was. Someone wanted her dead badly enough to take the head in her grave as proof of her death. Her Tretret commander could not help but notice her anxiety as they got closer. When they were in orbit over the city Alina came back on to the bridge to find double the security normally there. Long range scans did not pick up any other craft other than two shuttles and the space station within two million kilometers of the ship. The space debris could hide a dozen enemy ships easily and she commented on that to Danielle. While she handled other business Danielle had the debris scanned and anything that could conceal an unknown ship was eliminated. Five percent of the debris suddenly vanished from the Air Force Space Command Center scanners. Moment by moment more debris ceased to be there.

Back To A Beloved Place

THE LUNAR CITY was now like coming home. It never failed to amaze her when she was standing there in front of it. Older than the dinosaurs there was no doubt. A priority left as yet unfulfilled was to go to the library waiting in the cold darkness for someone to discover it's secrets. She could not read the languages but the Dofgrara could decipher them for her. Her mind was tempted by the universal mysteries just waiting on thousands of shelves. There were hundreds of thousands of volumes in that library and all she needed was one or two. She would have them put into protective containers and present them to the Prime Minister of England. Carbon dating would prove them older than anything or culture on earth. It would take years just to decipher the text using the most modern of computers. It would be almost impossible to do because of the certainity the languages in those volumes possessed no similarity what so ever to English. Dumb luck alone might show one close to a language spoken today. Initially languages of aincent cultures dating back thousands of years would be tried first. The languages of mathematics, chemistry and physics were possibile translation sources and would be investigated.

Walking to where her grave used to be there was now a jagged hole in the lunar soil. Wiliam found the dismembered remains of the body and hid them from the Captain. The remains were transported to the medical bay and reassembled for reburial. The head was still missing. In case they were being watched by someone they couldn't find the Captain was dressed as and positioned in the group as a junior officer would be. One of William's female team members was dressed and in the point of the Captain. The closeness of the Tretret to her was more convincing of who this person was. A burial party reinterred the remains with full honors of a command rank officer. As the burial progressed Alina's head was on a constant swivel movement as were most of the security teams. Nothing was seen by anyone and the scanners were blank on life signs. Scanners aboard the Long Island showed no other ships within eight million kilometers in any direction. Still Alina felt she was being watched. Unconciously she moved closer to her Tretret commander almost standing behind him. The commander pulled the false Captain into a closed circle to hide their true protection efforts. To the Captain it seemed the Tretrets surrounding her were larger than she remembered. She could not see anything beyond their backs because they were standing around her in an overlapping shield. Danielle kept a magnetic shield over them to prevent the Captain from being transported away.

Movement on the left brought the Tretret to instant alert. Confirmation of no life signs in the area didn't alleviate the tension. The Captain's own words came back to haunt her. The people of earth had to redefine their definition of what life was. Every inch of the lunar surface was being minutely scanned for anything out of place. Immediately apparent was that rocks were moving on their own. The Captain was instantly transported to the ship and a heavy security team met her on the pad. The safest place for her was on the bridge itself. Condition three was already initiated. That meant that the bridge and every access to it was sealed. Messages were sent to the New Iberia on a continuing basis to keep Captain Davis apprised of the situation. The moment Condition three was called and the Captain's jeopardy was relayed Captain Davis sent the New Iberia hurtling toward the Lunar City. Battle stations were ordered and five battle craft were prepared for immediate deployment as they neared the moon. Lomgren, because of their ultra sensitive hearing and sense of smell, were lined all along the hallway outside the bridge. Anything that they detected was by order of Danielle to be destroyed.

Danella and Danielle were in constant communication. Staerr and Tanya guaranteed communications channels remained open and prevented any interruptions. The Captain was sitting in her chair and all in front of her were Tretrets and a Medusa was close by her. They had become a standard bridge officer position they regarded as choice duty. Time and again their abilities had saved crewmembers and the ship itself from destruction. Alina trusted the Medusa implicitly and required their presence on the bridge. Screams from the hallway behind her brought her around in her chair. Two of the Tretrets moved between her and the doorway. Her commander walked into the hall to find a creature unknown to them lying dead. A Lomgran stood over it ready to attack again if necessary. Medics took the creature away for autopsy and detailed study. How it got aboard undetected was a major concern. The Medusa would find those who brought it aboard if it or they were still alive. Until he did the bridge remained sealed in case there were others. The Captain's quarters were scanned on the half hour for anything. Shape shifters were brought up to scan her quarters for other shapeshifters inside. None were located. Lomgren took rotating shifts in scanning her quarters to prevent one from missing something another did not detect. An intruder alert was sounded and Tretret and William's team members rushed to the transport pad area. Someone or something was trying to leave the ship.

The Medusan was very close behind them. On seeing the Medusan the intruder stabbed his own eyes. Tragically unnecessary since the medics had truth serums that worked just as well. What it, he or she knew was going to come out one way or the other. Lomgren were inches from them and gave the intruder no room for movement. He couldn't see them but he knew they were there. The medics were able to transplant artificial eyes in a matter of hours. As good if not better than their original eyes the Medusan still forced the truth from the creature. The Tarnet commander had arrived and was standing watching the questioning process. Captain Davis was still three ship periods away. This prisoner would be transported to the council for interrogation and judgement. The Volitny and the Bolterer ship were in orbit with the Long Island as well as three other council ships. Every ship had provided their own security teams to keep this thing alive, for now, and make sure nothing happened to it. Houston was trying to contact the Long Island and determine what was happening on the moon. Staerr was an expert at what is referred to as 'government speak' on earth.

Capable of forty minute diatribes that said absolutely nothing in it's entireity she was a valued diplomatic asset to the Captain. Tanya was as skilled as she and kept in practice dealing with interpanetary governing councils. The respect the governing councils had for the Captains was on record. The New Iberia was now entering orbit with the others. Captain Davis was stepping off the pad as Danielle welcomed him aboard. He was taken to the medical bay to see the intruder still alive. The Medusan had given the information needed against this thing's will. No surprise to anyone the Orion's were at the seat of the problem. Somehow someone helped them get back into space and the Captain was blamed for their misery. Captain Davis stepped up and said he was the one who started the trouble not Captain Grant. There was a problem with that tell him. Captain Grant had nothing to do with their current situation. Any further attack on Captain Grant would be answered with a full force retaliation by the New Iberia. Despite the influence of the Medusan the enemy responsible for the desecration of the Captain's grave remained a mystery.

Wiliam was standing by her as he usually did on the bridge. Alina turned to him and indicated she needed to talk to him privately. When Danielle tried to approach to listen in she was blocked by one of William's team. She told him," On earth there are what is called 'sleepers'. These are individuals that are agents for another government but don't know it themselves until a coded phrase is spoken then they carry out a specific mission. Many times without their concious will. This unknown enemy has very privileged information on the ships location and in particular her activities." She asked him if there might be a sleeper on the ship. They might even be on the bridge right now. A Medusan would be of no use because the individual is unaware of who they realy are. The thought that there was a mole for this avenging enemy was one of her bridge crew hurt her. Never before had she ever questioned the loyalty of her crew. Now she might have a spy with her and she had no idea who he, she or they were. She did not question her Tretrets. Danielle was definetly not an enemy agent. Staerr was as true as any one could be to her. William now searched the bridge crew with measured intensity. The Dofgrara had proved their loyalty to her countless times.

The Lomgren were incapable of treason against her. Her life had been threatened many times and too many of them had died defending her. Her Cerollon and Strefden were more like family than crew members. They would not betray her at any price. Someone who was always near her was an agent of this adversary. She told Staerr to set up a secure channel with the Tarnet commander and Captain Davis. Transfer it to her quarters. She told her Tretret commander to seal her quarters after she entered. When she walked in her door the entire area surrounding her quarters were evacuated including those areas above and below her quarters until the Captain allowed their return and all access was sealed. Four Tretrets and as many Lomgren were at her door or patrolling the hallway around her quarters. Not even Danielle had access to her unless there was an emergency requiring the Captain's attention. As per William's directives any time this occured there was a medical team within moments of her location. Even now a medical team was arriving to standby near her quarters.

Staerr told her that the secure channel was open and ready for her. Alina had to explain to the Tarnet Commander what a sleeper was but Davis already knew about them. The problem that Captain Davis now had to contend with was since he was aware of the Long Island's actions and in particular Alina's, the probability that an antagonist might be aboard his ship was high. Anyone on his ship that was found to be an enemy agent would face a furious unmerciful retribution. The Tarnet commander would do a security scan of his crew to eliminate any possibility of one being on his ship. The Planetary Council was also advised on closed channels of the situation that may be looming. Scans of their staff was mandatory at this point. No one would escape their attention. Three technicians failed to show up the following morning and could not be found. A ship left the planet the evening before without clearance and could not be located. This enemy was not just one or two individuals involved in this muderous conspiracy. Davis was scanning his bridge crew intently. He knew all of them quite well. Many had requested leaving the Long Island to serve with him again.

A Perilous Time Ahead

BEING THE CAPTAIN of a ship had it's privilages but they were out balanced by the responsibilities carried on his shoulders every day. The possibility of an enemy raising up was an ever present shadowy figure that could not be ignored. Wreckage was located by the Volitny ship within a days flight time from the Planetary Council's locale. The three technicians remains were among the debris. A secret is best kept when the fewest people know it. Even better when only one knows that secret. Debris would not be picked by the council's scanners. The pieces were too small to be a ship so they were eliminated by the scan. Autopsies would be done on the remains primarily to see if the identity of the life form could be determined. The cause of their deaths was apparent from the debris. They were never supposed to arrive at their rendezvous point alive. More secrets permanently silenced. The conference was still ongoing when the discovery was made but was determined to be noncritical in nature so the conference would not be hindered. Messages awaited the Captain when she returned to the bridge and the seal was recinded. Danielle looked at the Captain with uncertainity why she was excluded from the information. She was second in command and had to be aware of any and everything that might apply to her ability to command. Alina knew this and called her to her quarters to tell her what was happening. Excluding her from the conference was not intended to be a slight against her.

They walked out of her quarters and were in the hallway as they talked. No one was permitted near enough to hear them or able to read lips to understand what was said. Danielle would have to revise security protocols with William. Danella and she would have to conduct a closed communication to establish similar codes of operations on their respective ships. At Alina's request with Captain Davis a seperate channel was designated for Danella and Danielle's use for dialogue exclusively between them. What one second knew the other knew. It was a select license that neither had held before and they used it frequently. The autopsies showed nothing remarkable in the technician's planetary origin. Their deaths on the other hand held some interesting aspects. They were dead before the ship exploded. The poison used was still to be determined but it's virulence was fatal in the smallest of quantities. The bodies showed levels three hundred times the decreed lethal dose. Whoever these operatives worked for made sure they did not reveal any information. Whether they took the dosage intentionally or not was not a question deemed essential to know. William and Danielle as well as Danella and Michael were very closely aware of what they were facing. Section four on both ships were emptied and only the most violent would be held there and then dealt with as Wiliam or Michael determined.

With section four emptied the attacks against the Captain and the Long Island stopped for a short time. A sense of normalcy returned to the ship and the new security measures appeared to be working. Small skirmishes and incidents still occured but they were put down and the offenders dealt with summarily. Most of the time the offender's fate was not considered an issue to bother the Captain with. Only the loss of life of an offender was brought to her and Danielle's attention. Otherwise their sentence was determined by William or Michael and executed without delay. The prison colony on Targ was filling rapidly with those sent by William and Michael. An extremely inhospitable region of space Targ was synonymous with a living graveyard where the prisoner was sent and forgotten. Death was a preferable sentence to being inside Targ's gates. The number of Orion's sent there were increasing in number in no small part to the Tarnet Commander's actions.

Occasionally Alina would think of her home in Sherman, Texas wondering how things were now. It seemed ages since she had seen her family there. They believed her dead in the shuttle accident in space. The video showed her reaching for the shuttle bay door when the meteorite struck her helmet and then another striking her air pack and an explosion of gas into space. Somewhere in space they belived her body tumbled inexorably away from earth and any possibility of recovery. If they could see her now and her ship. Would they be proud of whom she had become or horrified at what her life had become. Unrecognizable to them they would not know her if she stood next to them. Except maybe to Linda her niece. That little treasure had abilities she could not explain. Linda had always demonstrated some type of second sight that marvelled everyone around her. How she missed her niece. Linda always made her laugh or did silly things that Alina would never forget. Someday she would have to return to Sherman, Texas just to see home again. Now she was having to deal with an enemy that killed it's own operatives or hired life forms to secrete themselves among her crew to kill her. The Lomgren seemed to know an enemy before she was aware they were even aboard. Usually she was advised after they were already dead by the medical bay. Several of these were being studied by the Planetary Council as they were hereto before unknown life forms. More than once the council had commented to the Captain on their preferring them to be alive when they arrived. Only so much could be learned from the dead. The Lomgren made no apologies for their killing an enemy.

She told Danielle to set course for World One Sam and wanted updates on Terra and Atlantis projects. Her house was in pristine condition and awaiting her return. There was something comforting about being on World One Sam she couldn't put her finger on but it was certainly there. The sound of the children playing across the lake was a welcome sound and helped ease her anxiety. Lately the last few days had taken quite a toll on her and she was hoping some time here would help rejuvenate her spirits. The New Iberia was at station Queen Three which was a surprise for her. Several council ships were amassing at Queen Three and David Four. In seperate quadrants there were at least five hour jump flights from another. Communications were garbled or overlapping each other which was unusual. Preparing to return to the Long Island she ordered an increased alert status on her arrival. Only having four days on World One was still a welcome break. Time to get back to work. Point Nora Six was about halfway between the two quadrants. She would assume a watch and see at Nora Six and go where she would be most needed. In the mean time any upgrades would be done and the star navigation charts would be checked and then checked again for accuracy. Staerr was busy monitioring the communications and the Dofgrara were monitoring adjacent communication channels for anything unusual that might indicate ongoing problems the ship might have to deal with.

Danielle was doing a weapons systems check as William was doing his usual security checks on all decks. The galley was busy preparing the

Captain's lunch and would have it ready when she arrived at the Captain's table. This time she wanted it brought to the bridge not feeling comfortable leaving right now. Things on the bridge were heating up as the messages between the two sectors were becoming more insistent on immediate attention required. Turning to her Tretret commander she said she wanted four battle craft standing by for immediate deployment. Also at least two of the scout ships should be made ready at her command. Place medical bay on alert for possible casualities and make secure all engine and weapons control compartments from intruders. Set Condition three immediately. As she was saying these things additional Tretrets and Lomgren came onto the bridge. The Medusan was ever present beside her. Danielle and Starr were going from station to station checking their operational readiness. Alina ordered a star navigational fix and fastest course and speed to Queen Three or David Four put into helm computers. The ship was at readiness. Weapons were ready, life support was double checked, a company of Cerollon and Strefden were assembled and the Tretret commander was following each and every situational update from both sectors. This was the first time Alina had wished she was two persons on two ships.

Neither the Tarnet Command ship or the New Iberia were unknown to battle situations. Increasing numbers of councils ships were being deployed to both quadrants. Danielle and Danella kept their select channel open following each ship's condition closely. Captain Davis knew that Alina was not in the thick of this one and that had some comfort to it. The situation in David Four was closing down and Alina ordered the Long Island to Queen Three at best speed. Scannners aboard were looking at everything it picked up. If there was a question a Dofgrara looked at each individual unknown contact. They were the ones that found the shrouded ships from the communications that were being exchanged from points of empty space. Danielle targeted them and at her command the ships were erased in momentary issues of light. Two more were located and they too were removed from the fight. The Long Island was picked up by the enemy ships and they turned to run. The battle craft stopped their flight by disabling their weapons and engine sections. The enemy would stand in judgement by the Planetary Council. Since these were alive they would willingly or unwillingly provide information as needed.

When the Long Island was in transport range several Sinefors were transported into the enemy ships central computer centers. They disabled their self destruct and vital ship control systems without the enemy ever knowing they were there until it was too late. When the Long Island's crew breached the ships hulls the crew tried to destroy their own ships to no avail. The crews and their ships would be taken to the Planetary Council to be dealt with there. Alina tired of these charades by her enemy wished them all a suffering death. She was so disgusted by all these events that Alina put these creatures out of her mind and returned to her bridge. On entry Danielle gave her a ship's condition and readiness report. Three of the battle craft crew members returned with minor scrapes and bruises and that was the extent of injuries to her crew. The enemy's planetary origins were yet to be identified. More than half suffered crushing injuries from Tretret fists, broken extremities and severe concussions. Five died from Lomgren bites and Strefden blades. She called the three with minor scrapes to the bridge to thank them for jobs well done. All three had pleased looks on their faces having been able to finally engage an invisible foe. Those that survived would not forget this fight any time soon nor would they ever underestimate Captain Grant again.

The Long Island hosted the Tarnet Commander and Captain Davis for a dinner situational conference. It was well into the evening time periods when the other Captains returned to their ship. Alina was exhausted and when the normal time of her awakening came about Danielle let her sleep. It was the fourth time period of the day watch when Alina came onto the bridge rested and feeling much better. Daniellle told her she ordered her left alone to rest. Alina thanked her and after a quick briefing on the events from the evening before and into today Alina was ready to continue her day. Skirmishes by the prisoners aboard the Tarnet Commanders ship resulted in more injuries to them and no injuries to the Tarnet guards. As of yet their origin was not being divulged. Several of the prisoners on a Volitny ship were reportedly injured when they ran into ship's bulkheads quite forcefully. Alina sarcastically thought accidents happen and thought no more of them. The desire to see the Prime Minister again had been on the Captain's mind for some time. She asked Danielle if there was pressing business in this sector yet to be done or calibrations of navigation systems requiring their remaining here. Daniellle answered no to both questions and said they were clear and free to navigate any course the Captain desired. The course to earth sector was always kept in the helm's computer.

"Set course for earth specifically England. Best course and speed. Jump capability is authorized." Danielle said, "Right away Captain. Expect earth sector in fifteen time periods. Will advise when we are one time period away". Without being told to Staerr knew to contact the Prime Minister's office before arrival. She also let Tanya know of their planned destination so Captain Davis was aware. It was made plain to Danella and Danielle that Alina was very important to him. The secure channel for Danielle and Danella had been getting a lot of use since implementation. A license both felt long needed by them. There was nothing one did not know that the other did not and it served to allow both seconds to conduct operations simultaneously with precision. "Danielle you have the bridge. I am going to walk around a bit, there are several sections I should check on while I have time". As always Tretrets and Cerollons accompanied her everywhere. Strefden were very close by ready at a moment's cry to fight. Lomgrens always were in front of her. The first obstacles any threat had to overcome to reach her.

Alina was talking with her Tretret commander casually and was discussing things that she thought he needed to know like specific codes that until now he did not have access to. He was being given more and more knowledge continuously it seemed any of which may be critical to his protecting her. He possessed information that Captain Davis's lead commander did not. At the Captain's orders he was given access to all parts of the ship that Danielle and she possessed which in essence meant all of the ship. Several areas were blockaded from any access. She asked Danielle why these were closed to her. She was told they should not be closed off at all. Turning to her commander she said, "Find me a way through that." He pulled her back a short distance then had the barricade barraged by attack weapons from the Cerollons. Firecrews were standing by just in case. William and half a dozen of his team were ready to storm into the barricaded areas. Lomgren were prepared to meet anything they encountered on the other side of those barricades. At a moments consideration she had engineering and Sinefors available if needed.

Is There No End To Battle

A FTER RECENT EVENTS there would be hell to pay on who ever was hidden behind here. Fourteen Tretrets were standing between the unknown and the Captain. Watching the Lomgren she saw them looking above them following something or someone. She alerted her commander and she was immediately transported to the bridge. This was their war and there would be no quarter here. The Cerollon would be the first to engage this unknown. Strefden were ready with their weapons to impale anything trying to drop on them. William and his team had split into two teams. The first to breach the blockaded areas and the second to confront the enemy that was still to be discovered. On advising of situation on the Long Island Captain Davis had Michael check the corresponding areas on the New Iberia. As feared they too were blockaded. The retribution facing this enemy was going to be horrific and without any mercy whatsoever. Access to the bridges of both ships were sealed. The war began with blockades being melted where they stood before and would end when all the enemy was destroyed. The Tarnet command ship was facing a similar situation. Somehow this unknown got aboard the council's top three ships undetected, sealed off the areas they wanted and were prepared to keep them. Messages to the council were flashed on emergency channels to all ships and council facilities.

This enemy more than any other before presented the gravest danger to the council save for the virus carriers. That it may be the virus carriers seeking vengeance was not dismissed. Holding his teams back William ordered the compartments blocked flooded with radiation from the engine section. No life form could survive such massive doses of radiation. Even in protective gear the engineers could stay no more than seven minutes in the engine section before they absorbed a fatal dose. This would be a continous flooding of radiation for a minimum of fifteen minutes. Anything inside was dead long before that time was up. Although no one else could hear inside the compartment the Lomgren had no trouble hearing the screams of agony and suffering taking place within. They stated the screams had stopped and there were no more sounds from the compartments. The areas would be permanantly sealed because of radiation contamination. The dead would remain inside as radioactive as their environment for thousands of years. To ships as large as the New Iberia and the Long Island three sections was negligable in space lost. To other smaller council ships a single sections space lost was catastrophic to operations. Radiation was not the answer to their dilemnas.

The New Iberia and the Long Island both offered to send troops to strengthen the other ships compliments as needed. The Cerollons were indeed the first to meet this unknown and they were the last thing many saw before they died. No mercy was to be given this enemy and none was given. The battle raged on in the hallways of the New Iberia for more than a ship's time period and when it was over none of the enemy survived. Two Cerollons were lost along with one Tretret and one Strefdan in the melee. Lomgren seemed to take particular delight in attacking this enemy. Their bite killing them in a few seconds before they could recover to fight back. Just before they died they discovered hiding from the Lomgren was a lost effort. The New Iberia was still more than twenty time periods from earth sector. A return to the lunar city cemetery was necessary to lay their honored dead to rest. The enemy's remains were unceremoniously ejected into space like garbage. Such a visit's reason was not the case for the Long Island. The unknown in the flooded compartments would stay there forever. End of problem.

Alina was looking forward to some time back on earth. This time, as she had promised herself, she would go back to Sherman, Texas. The Prime Minister was joyous as always to see her. He told her Edinburgh was becoming the world's center for advanced medical research. Even NASA had come to learn and take back the technology they had always wanted. Alina said almost under breath, "All they had to do was follow my instructions." He heard her but said nothing in reply. The tabloids were reporting every facet of falsehood about the Captain and the Prime Minister imaginable. A thought crossed her mind that maybe the tabloid reporters should be transported inside the sealed compartments but then dismissed it as over reacting. Though, she reminded herself, it was not impossible. The world had changed in a very short time with the advisors program. Space technology had leaped ahead hundreds of years in a matter of days. Maybe, the thought crossed Alina's mind, the progress was too fast. She doubted that any country was able to handle the new technology wisely. But, as she noted, the progress was not enough. Many countries still had massive hunger and many still needed fresh water to drink. Space technology was all well and good but hungry children were more important and came first.

Every where she looked there was something about the Centaurs. Photos of the creatures that were in Sanwich was in a book that sold out as soon as it was put on the shelves. People were curious about the life out there in space. They had pictures of these creatures and they wanted to know about more life forms. The publics curiousity was insatiable about the universe they shared. Travel agencies ached to be able to sell trips to other worlds. University research departments were seeking passage on any ship that would accept them going anywhere off the planet. An unquenchhable hunger to learn more about this universe teeming with life had overwhelmed the advisors programs. Additional advisors were always being needed to quell this hunger. Classes held by advisors were packed to maximum capacity and more often over booked in numbers. Model companies had models of the Long Island, New Iberia, the Volitny ship, Bolterer ship and the Tarnet command ship on hobby store shelves. They could not keep up with the demand customers were wanting. Anything space related was in high demand. Television shows and movies were changing to reflect the public's desire for more about space and it's wonders waiting to be discovered. Jokingly the Prime Minister said, "This is your doing you know." She was walking past a clothing store and exact copies of her gown from the ball were on display. Her flight suit was replicated in exact detail in another store and a hair salon was offering a Captain's cut to it's fashionable customers.

An Enemy Identified

D ANIELLE CUT IN on her reflective time and advised that the council had identified the planetary origin of the enemy. It was previously unknown to the council. Now with the aid of Medusans and serums designed to extract information they were learning much more about this new culture. The planet in sector Echo Five was about eighteen hours with jump capability from point Queen One. That put it about six light years from earth. Why the attacks was still being extracted in slow detail. A Conteneran ship arrived at the planet and recovered the head stolen from the Captain's grave. It would be a while before all that was hidden would be brought to light. Now the Captain felt she had been released from the terror she had lived with for all these weeks. The greatest feeling of redemption washed over her and happiness that her crew would no longer be in jeopardy. When she transported aboard the Long Island she was greeted with thundering applause and congratulations of her victory. She felt truly relieved and relaxed for the first time in a very long time. Danielle said that she was sorry to ruin her joy but the New Iberia was enroute to the lunar city with her dead from the battle in her hallways. The Tretrets were able to use full power in their strikes and the Lomgren were watching, sniffing the air and listening as they went through the previously barricaded sections. It was not over for them just yet.

Turning to the Prime Minister she told him the New Iberia was returning to the cemetery with dead from a battle aboard the ship and that she had to go. He asked if he could accompany her and if the Captain would allow some of his staff to be pallbearers. Alina had Danielle contact the New Iberia and ask that very question to Captain Davis.

When the New Iberia arrived in orbit over the lunar city the Prime Minister's team were suited up and ready to carry their burdens to the cemetery. Being on the moon was becoming routine for some of his staff. For the Royal Marines it was a new experience. As the Royal marines set foot on the moon for the first time all about them was desolation. The city itself loomed in front of them enormous in scope and the tower pinnacle was too high for them to see. The New Iberia's crew was waiting for them to retrieve the caskets now waiting at the base of the Captain's yacht ramp. Captain Grant's honor ceremony was conducted and the Marines picked up the caskets. Even at one third weight the Tretret were heavy and required eight Marines to carry. As the burial cremony was completed the Captain went to specific graves and wiped dust away from name markers and patted them gently. The Prime Minister watched her move from grave to grave and felt this woman was still as mysterious to him as the first time he had seen her. It was her favorite place and saddest place for the Captain. She walked among the rows of the dead laid here at her feet and paused at this grave or that and touched the name marker there softly. It did not ecscape the members of her crew that the Captain was soft enough to remember her crew in this maner. How many millinium times millinium had they remained here in this place inactive until Captain Davis reactivated them. Their own culture did not care enough to seek them out and recover them. Here this small human honored all her crew, living and dead. When they believed her dead the seperation from her was overwhelming to many and some could not be consoled. Now she had returned to them and the enemy that caused all this misery was being dealt with as harshly as council law allowed.

Engineers from every council ship were tearing the enemy ships apart and examining every aspect of them. Their weapons were being torn down and left in scrap piles. Their main computer systems were being looked at in intimate detail by Sinefors and all the information in the memory banks was downloaded onto council intelligence computers. It would take months to go through it all. The reason for the attacks was still eluding the council investigators. The head from the grave was reburied with the body and given final honors again. As they prepared to leave this place the Royal Marines gave the Captain honors of their own. She thanked them and had photos that would never see the light of day taken with them. The memories of this day would remain with the Marines all their lives. Of course they could not speak of this to anyone as they were sworn to secrecy. As they looked around for the last time wondering at the origin of the lunar city they were standing in the hangar building they left earlier in the day. As evening settled in and the moon rose in the sky the Marines had a different aspect of this neighbor above them. They would never see it the same way as before. The sky was different on the moon they could see planetoids, comets, and meteors they could not on earth. There were so many wonders right in front of them they could not put into words no matter how they tried.

Yes Alina was a beautiful woman with the softness of a lover but the Captain was ever present and held her aloof from those around her. Her ship and crew came first and for this the Prime Minister was always concious of and respected. William approached her and said that the prisoners in section four demanded to see her and wanted a pardon, actually demanded it. She said very coarsely to him, "Tell them their demands are denied. And William I want them off this ship. I will not tolerate their presence any longer. Remove them at first opportunity". William acknowledged her orders and in moments without space suits they were materialized on the moon surface hundreds of miles from the cemetery. Section four was once again empty and the cells were being cleaned out prepared for the next guest list. The legend, if that could be stated about the Long Island, was ever growing. The Captain, at least by name, was known by every planetary member of the council. This was their first contact with humans and she and Captain Davis were always finding some remarkable resolve to a sitiuation. Most cultures in the council had no idea what an 'imagination' was or understood how humans used it. It was an interesting quality however, baffling but interesting quality. This imagination allowed humans to see the outcome possiblities of a situation and plan for them long in advance.

Danielle was going station to station on the bridge when the Captain entered to the customary call "Captain on the bridge." She asked her for ships report and condition as she usually did first. The ship was at readiness for navigation and all systems were normal. "I am going back down to the planet Danielle. My hometown is Sherman, Texas and I want to see it again." "Very well Captain, enjoy your time there." When she materialized about a half mile from town there were seven with her. Two very large men and several smaller men with walking sticks. The humidity and heat was oppressive at first but the familiar smells were wonderful to her senses. The dogs with her were always in front of her but appeared well heeled to observers. The onslaught of smells that hit them was a curious blend of many unknowns.

They heard mice and scorpions in the brush and snakes were close by and the buzz of their tails said don't come closer. They smelled coyotes that had passed through here recently as well as the smell of people walking the road. Lots of humans had passed through here recently. They smelled the liquor of empty bottles and wrappers discarded by the roadside.

A blip of a police siren told her they were not alone and the officer approached her. He asked for identifications from all of them which they did not have. The sharp sting of a needle in his arm closed the conversation for that evening. His patrol partner found him in his car unresponsive to stimulus of any type. He would wake in a few hours his head feeling like it was burning but it would pass with no after effects. Massive sized tracks were near by as well as dog prints. These dog prints were unfamiliar to him. He had dogs all of his life but these didn't look normal. These dogs had only two pads on their feet and five claws. There were indications, though the officer could not be sure, of three claws on the back of each foot. The Lomgran would be happy to explain that but he doubted the officer could handle a dog speaking to him. Sherman had certainly changed in the years she had been away. A van provided their necessary transportation needs. The driver was drunk sleeping it off in the back. A Strefdan made sure he did not wake up at an inconvienent time. The same type of needle injection kept him quiet and compliant. When the driver did awake his van was parked about forty miles outside Sherman. His head felt like it was on fire. What ever he drank last night he would avoid the next time.

The home she knew was owned by someone else now and the yard was a trash dump. Alina had taken pride in keeping the yard neat and tidy when she had the house. Very disappointing to see now. Someone from the house came out with a shotgun to shew them away and learned the power behind a Tretret fist the hard way. The shotgun barrel was twisted in an impossible shape lying on the ground next to him. Two fractures of his skull and multiple concussions were the reward for his aggression. When questioned about what he remembered all he could see was this massive fist coming at him and then lights out. His back was indented in the side of his house where he ended up after being hit. That was about twenty feet behind him. A single punch knocked him all across his yard to smash into his house. Whatever did this was of a monstrous size. A drug addict tried to rob the

Captain and the bite of a Lomgran ended his addiction. His body was found by a passerby jogging early in the morning.

Sherman, Texas PD was trying to figure out what was going on when news of the addicts body came in. The toxin delivered by a bite from an animal that appeared to be a dog was found by the medical examiner. No dog or canine he knew of was venomous. This species was definetly venomous and it's toxicity was devastating. Survivability of this canine's bite was one hundred percent fatal in a matter of seconds. Two more men known to be cartel were brought in and had identical wounds as this man. A man was delivered to the hospital emergency room with injuries from a crushing blow to his chest. The bruise from impact was the width of his chest. He was complaining of not being able to breathe. Truly disappointed by what she was finding she wanted to go where her family used to live and found them home looking into the sky with telescopes. Her aunt said, "Somewhere up there Alina is tumbling through space." Tears were evident in her mother's eyes and that tore Alina apart she couldn't stay any longer. It hurt to much to see her mother crying.Before she was far away one of the Lomgren told her that her mother's heart was damaged. The medics could help her. She would not walk away from her mother, not now.

Calling Danielle she ordered the medics to stand by for emergency patient with cardiac difficulty. Turning around she walked up to her mother and said she could help her. Her mother did not recognize her face but this woman's voice was familiar. In the space of a breath her mother was standing on the transport pad. She kept being told "Let me help you, I can help you" over and over. Men that appeared to be doctors were all around her. There were other things here too, things she could not recognize. Her heart rate rapidly rose and this woman said it's ok they are here to help you too. Something about her voice was so familiar so she was calm. An angel stood by her as well as a giant of a man. There was a centaur here too. Where was she? On earth the Sherman police received a report of the kidnapping of a seventy year old woman by a young woman and a giant with her. Their mother had just disappeared literally. A creature the size of a grizzly bear came up to this woman and said all engineering sections were ready. There was a man with a long spear or something standing behind her like a guard. Finally she knew why the voice was familiar. This woman was her daughter Alina. Raising her hand from her bed she asked if she was her Alina. The woman nodded her head yes and the emotions overwhelmed both of them. The woman explained there was much she had to tell her but right now these doctors were going to repair her heart. She would see her in a short while. Darkness slowly closed in and her mother was taken into surgery. The Captain was at the Captain's table talking with Danielle and William when she recieved a message her mother was being taken into a recovery area. There were no complications and the surgery went well.

Sherman police were still trying to piece together all these events. They appeared to be connected but they were not sure how yet. Three dead from the bite of a venomous dog. Several men brought in from crushing blows to the head or chest. One patient in a traction splint because he smashed into his house after being hit by a single blow. A seventy year old woman kidnapped by a younger woman and a giant. A police officer drugged on the highway and another man wakes up miles from Sherman with similar complaints. The toxic screen did show an unknown drug in both their systems but the chemical composition was not terrestrial in nature. The sheriff's department had been alerted and the Texas DPS was already involved. The result of non terrestrial chemical composition was automatically FBI jurisdiction.

When Alina's mother opened her eyes she was right there beside her. There were so many questions she had but didn't know where to begin. Alina said, "Let me show you mom. This will answer most of your questions." She introduced the medical staff who were android as was Danielle, her second in command and Wiliam, her security chief. "The creatures next to me are Tretrets. Their primary function is to protect the Captain, that's me and Danielle. There are more than three hundred fifty different life forms aboard. And all except the Sinefors can communicate with us. Even the Lomgren", she indicated the dog next to her, "can communicate with you." The Lomgran by her mother welcomed her aboard. She indicated the winged creature near them and said, "These are Cerollons. The one's here with long sticks are Strefden. The grizzly you saw in the medical bay is an Amdor. They are the engineers aboard the Long Island. That is the name of my ship." All of this was just proving too much for her mother to take in at one time. Her daughter was alive and the Captain of a ship filled with other wordly creatures. The medic pushed the gurney back toward the medical bay.

By the time morning tones sounded Alina was already in the medical bay talking with her mother. She emphasized that she could not tell anyone she was still alive or who and what she is. It was enough that Alina was alive. She would keep the secret always. A creature must be almost nine feet tall stood near her and Alina introduced the Tarnet Central Command fleet commanding officer to her mother. There were creatures that she had never imagined but were calling her daughter the Captain, can you believe it, they were happy her mother was going to be ok. Danielle introduced the commanders of the Volitny, Bolterer, Conteneran and Strayler ships. She was finally introduced to her daughter's greatest friend Captain Davis. His ship was the New Iberia? There is a place in Louisiana with the same name and it dawned on her that was why it was so named. In two days she would be returned to earth able to function as she did before her heart condition. In the mean time on earth there were lines of people going through the areas around Sherman scanning for any hint of where Mrs. Grant had disappeared to. Her heart condition was of vital concern to them.

As Alina entered the bridge with her mother next to her she heard, "Captain on the bridge" called out. What wonders she was seeing on the view screen. The ship had moved to point Queen One and was standing by to assist a ship coming from the dark space with food and medical assistance if they were still alive. The ship was a virus carrier ship and Danielle ordered it immediately destroyed. Turning to Staerr she asked her to explain to her mother what she was seeing on the screen. Her mother was mesmerized by all presented before her. She was the first person outside the crew to see this part of space. The constellations and the moons and the colors of the creation of star systems took her breath away. There to the right was a comet whose core was iron and would be near earth in about eight hundred years. The Captain ordered a position overlay on the screen to get celestial position. The overlay showed which planets were near by and which moons was close to them, comets, asteroids and meteorites were all marked clearly for the Captain to make a decision. Her mother asked why the ship was destroyed and was told the ship was recognized as one that had a destructive virus carrier aboard. The Captain had the ships position marked for reference. The crew was not alive as the ship design was one hundred years old at least.

Her mother felt the change in aspect of the ship as it turned about to a new heading. In nine ship periods her mother would be back in her kitchen. Instead they would put her near a rescue station outside Sherman. She would be examined and found in surprisingly good health. She would not remember where she had been. There would just be images. What she did remember was that her daughter Alina was alive and somewhere in space the Captain of a massive ship. Now when she looked through the telescope it was not to grieve where Alina might be. It was to wonder where she is now in that amazing ship she commanded. On the Sunday morning exactly five days since her disappearance Alina's mother was found walking along the highway eleven miles from Sherman. She appeared disheveled and dirty as was expected but was not in any physical distress for a woman with a heart condition. She was in surprisingly good spirits for a woman missing several days. Her children rushed to her side as soon as they heard of her being found. She said she had talked to Alina and as soon as she said it regretted it.

They attritbuted it to a mother still grieving for her daughter lost in space. Something happened to her that no one could explain. Her heart was repaired but there were no scars from cardiac surgery. It was as if her heart miraculously healed itself.

The Long Island in lunar geosynchronous orbit was cloaked from earth's radar and scanners. The lunar scan satellite that had catastrophically failed before began transmitting again. It's images were clearer and sharper than before but it's position was not where intended. It's cameras were pointed to a section two hundred kilometers above the lunar city. The images it was sending back was of gun emplacements in eight different locations on crater rims. Control buldings were clearly in the images and tracks from vehicles to and from the buildings were evident. Why the satellite stopped was no longer the primary question to be answered. Alina intentionally planned for this mystery to be discovered. The emplacements abandoned for decades would still be the overwhelming objects of investigation for years by earth's military services. The discovery would take away from her presence as she explored the city's vast library. She took more volumes from the library and transported them To Ten Downing Street in London. Their discovery there would cause a furor by the Royal family as to why they were not being included in these affairs. A semi honest lie of an excuse would be created as an answer. Such is the basis of diplomacy.

Danielle was scanning the earh's stations and thought the Captain would be interested in one report in particular. Her mother was being interviewed and stated she didn't remember much of what happened to her in that time. As to her heart she had no clue how or why it healed. This was a lie of course but to keep her secret it was justified. Her family could not exlain her sudden interest in obtaining a model of the Long Island but it seemed important to her so they bought one. One of her grandchildren assembled it for her and the model was prominently dispalyed on the mantle. Occasionally she planted a kiss with the tip her hand on the model or pat it gently. Very strange behavior for a woman her age. Her health was wonderously so much better and she was doing things she had not able to for many years. Her mind was sharp and clear. She would sing more when she moved about the house and when the telescope was used she wanted it trained on the southern hemisphere of the moon. Her enemy still maintained silence despite the drugs and Medusan influences in interrogation. Their anatomical structure was placed into the medcal computers to be used as identifying markers when next encountered.

Memories Of Better Times

ALINA WAS HAVING dinner with Captain Davis their conversation was spoken at a level only a few could hear. Five of the security force stood between them and anyone getting close enough to hear what was being said. The Lomgran could hear and they would not repeat what was learned. They had the Captain's trust in confidential matters and they would not betray that faith. Seven times they had been predisposed to reveal information at a critical time and kept their silence. The two Captains walked through the halls of the New Iberia but even here the team surrounding them kept a watchful but respectful distance. Danella was present with them and was a very involved part of the conversation. Her android mind was converting information into aspects that her computer would accept. Since she never forgot anything she heard or learned the information was stored for future use. There were things that she and Danielle would need to talk about on their closed channel. When the Captains returned to the bridge Danella was already making necessary changes in the navigation system preparing to initiate orders that would forthcoming.

Alina walked onto her own bridge to find similar preperations already in place awaiting her orders. First there was the matter of section four to be considered. A matter of several inmates being displaced without the Captain's input. As William explained to the Captain none of the inmates displacements were done against her knowledge. She had expressed her desire that the inmates be sent off the ship at first opportunity. In William's interpretation that meant immediately regardless of where they were. Transported into empty space or miles from the lunar city cemetery her orders were followed exactly. Alina was going to say something in response but reconsidered her words. William followed her orders to the exact letter of statement. From now on she would specify her commands. Inmates lives literally depended on what she reputed. There were, as she thought about it, more than a few that got their just punishment. The Planetary Council did not have any condemnation of William's interpretation of the Captain's orders. She was in the Captain's chair and had been quiet for some while when Danielle's calling her name seeped through the flow of her memories. She turned to respond and Danielle was pointing to something on the view screen.

Wreckage In Space

THE WRECKAGE OF several ships were tumbling vicarioulsy through the sector they were in. The Captain wanted any information on the ships as far as identification that could be ascertained. She ordered that concurring messages be sent to the New Iberia and all council ships in the area. She asked if the computer could determine how many ships were shown. Staerr reported that it appeared to be five ships represented. Alina asked if the number of crews lost could be determined. Not at this point she was told. The wreckagwe was at least one week old. One week could mean their destructor could still be nearby. She spoke to Danielle and said she didn't think a condition alert was necessary right now. She did want, however, an increased level of alert on the ship. Within minutes the front of the bridge area was lined with extra members of William's team, four additional Tretrets were present near the Captain and the Medusan was, as ever, near by. Two additional Lomgren were sitting on either side of the Captain's chair. Information was slow to come in but the ships appeared to be council members in origin.

The New Iberia was coming into the sector as was the Volitny ship. None of the responding crews recognized the markings on the wreckage. There were no life signs as was expected, the bodies of the crews could be anywhere flying through space. No doubt the bodies would be discovered over time. If they were an unknown species tying them to the wreckage would be a diffucult puzzle to solve. At the Captain's request a team of investigators would be dispatched to the Long Island to determine exactly what had been found. Investigators representing more than a dozen council member planets began to arrive in staggered order. Ships bay number eight had been set aside for the origin of the ship's remains to be discovered. Sinefors and Long Island engineers were already searching through what was already aboard. Finding what piece belonged to what ship would take time to sort out. Computer components brought to light in the wreckage were more confusing. Technology of this measure was unknown to council scientists. The first to come to Alina's mind were the Gray's.

She had seen, to her disgust, the Grays, Greens and the reptilians. The Nordics were closer in appearance to humans than most life forms she had met. Slight in appearance the women were a half inch taller than the male with both slightly under six feet tall. The men are broad shouldered and physically powerful despite their viewed stature. From the Antarran system their presence on earth had been known by the worlds governments since September of nineteen forty three. In the time since that date one hundred sixty more species had come to light. Numerous programs to surreptitiously confirm and deny their presence had risen and fallen. Project Blue Book and Majestic to name but two. How many more could only be surmised. Many more than ever concieved of no doubt and there would always be others. The advisor program put most if not all but the most secretive in the light. Even these were overshadowed by the discoveries made every day in Miami, Edinburgh, Bonn and other world capitols.

Alina was in conference in her quarters with Captain Davis when the general alarm on the ship sounded. Rushing to the bridge she walked into an orchestrated chaos. Staerr reported a class one distress had been recieved from a council transport ship two hours from the Long Island's position. The ship had minimal armament and at last transmission was going into a core jump to avoid capture. The image of what was left after a core jump was not a pleasant one. If a core jump was initiated the enemy was known and there was no option to stop them. Scanners were at full search distances and should have picked up a second ship. All the scanners were showing was the transport. She motioned Danielle to her and whispered something to her. Danielle went to the weapons console and readjusted the weapons trace scanners. The residue of a weapons blast was detected and by correlating trace with time passed and probable course and speed of vessel they were able to calculate the enemy ships current position. A twenty percent intensity setting with full torpedo spread hit something disabling it temporarily. Battle craft were already in position to breach the hull and board the ship. The transport was a graveyard of unrecognizable masses everywhere. The bodies of the crew were indescernable from the cargo. A core jump is an absolute last resort because no one and nothing survives it's violence.

The transport ship would be towed to the Planetary Council planet and they could deal with the carnage there. Those still alive aboard the attacking ship were quickly overpowered by the boarding crew. Sorian and Orion were among the captured crew which was a surprise. The Tarnet Commander was quick to seize the Orion before any one else could. As for the Sorian's the Volitny crew took them off the ship with considerable resistance. The remaining crew members were of unknown species. It was likely the Orion's would never see the approaching day. The Sorian's would feel the pangs of a Council prison farm. The new lifeforms were another matter. Why the intrusion into Council space by these species was unknown. The New Iberia and the Long Island would continue to be the vanguards of the fleet, the most feared and despised as well. The Tarnet Commander and Captain Davis were talking walking the halls of the New iberia about the arrival back into space by the Orion's. They were a problem that refused to go away. A survey from space of the new Orion planet showed high industrial capacity and space vehicle building facilities were apparent. Someone was helping them with considerable technology advancements. A war may yet be necessary to end their threat to the council members.

Mysterious Happenings

C APTAIN DAVIS WALKED onto the bridge to find all in complete bedlam. Danella was rushing from station to station checking readings at stations. Alert had not been sounded but the weapons were online and fully charged. Turning to him she reported that they had unconfirmed reports that the Long Island was adrift and that possibly a core jump was initiated. Readings showed the ship listing at six degrees with no attempt to correct. Life signs were negligable and there were no answers to hails. There were five battle ships of indeterminate origin closing on the Long Island. Tanya was repeatedly sending messages to the Long Island with no response. Aspect of the ship was at eleven degrees down angle. Captain Davis had hoped he would never have to send this message but instructed Tanya to send Red Two catagory message to the Planetary Council with possible loss of the Long Island. Within minutes scanners on the New Iberia was picking up a number of Council ships closing on the Long Island's location. The five battle ships were slowing as they neared the ship. They began to take up positions to prepare to board the Long Island. Not in Davis's lifetime would that be allowed. Targeting the closest ship the New Iberia fired a full spread of torpedoes at full power. The ship disappeared in five flashes of blue white light.

The others now aware of the New Iberia were sending frantic messages of non aggression. The Volitny and and two Borerra ships took attack positions around the remaing battle ships. The approach of the New Iberia was an ominous presence closing on the Long Island. Constant messages sent between the council ships were sent on open channels so that the battle ships knew exactly where they stood. Davis steeled himself for what he would find when he boarded. The Tarnet commander stood next to him on the transport pad when he materialized on the Long Island. The hallways were filled with the bodies of the crew. It wasn't until they checked them they discovered the life forms were still breathing. The androids were as statues and unresponsive to commands. The bridge was intact with no sign of intrusion. Alina was collapsed in her chair. Breathing but otherwise unresponsive. Captain Davis acting on impulse alone entered a typed command into the ship's helm computer and the ship began to correct it's attitude to normal. Transported to the New iberia medical bay Aina was put into a critical care unit. Sinefor's were sent aboard the Long Island to reactivate the androids on the ship and the engineers were awakened by the medics. Danielle was standing next to the weapons console as if she was trying to do something frozen in time. She was reactivated by the Sinefor as well. Almost immediately she looked around for the Captain. Not finding her she started to look for her. A medic told her she was aboard the New Iberia in the medical bay and was safe.

Captain Davis asked her if she was able to command the ship. Danielle assured him she was and began to check all ships systems and crew conditions. The Tretret normally beside the Captain were awakened and when their heads were clear demanded to be near the Captain. William was reactivated and was extremely violent when he was. An adjustment to his processor corrected his aggression. Those in section four were not awakened. Instead William ordered them to remain as they were. Tretrets near the Captain were never more than a few inches away even when medics were caring for her. Captain Davis and the Tarnet Commander began an investigation as to what would cause this situation. William and five of his team was sent to the power section on the ship. There were eight lifeforms very much active in the engine section. Before they could capture them they transported off the ship. A scan for cloaked ships returned no results. Whoever, whatever this attacker was would not be known. Days after she was under medical care Alina woke on her own. Weak and confused she was not able to walk unassisted. Her Tretret guards were there for any need she had and always near her. Engineers and Sinefor's were unable to determine why the crew was affected as they were. The technology required to do this was far above anything they were aware of. As advanced as their own technology levels were this weapon was unknown. The effect of the weapon was obvious but how it worked or it's composition was not known. Why it would show a core jump initiation did not make any sense.

Alina's hair had gray highlights in it that were not there before. It was several days before Alina walked back onto the bridge unassisted. Danielle was beside her when she entered and after asking if she was OK gave her a toned down report of ships condition and crew status. The view screen showed the lunar city. Alina asked how many were lost during the attack. Six had been laid to rest on the morning before. Alina ordered a battle craft prepared and her flight suit readied for her. As the door of the battle craft opened on the lunar surface the Captain rose from the craft's ramp and slowly flew toward the cemetery. Six new graves joined those already there. She looked at the names on the markers and knew all of them. Most of the dead were Tretret which told her that they had fought with their enemy. They died protecting her. She wanted to know how they died and had the autopsy reported to their quarters. Instead to protect her the lead physician reported to ther quarters and told her how they died. Without being to graphic he described some of their injuries. Tears flowed from her eyes as she listened. Her sorrow and regret at the Tretret's loss did not escape Danielle or the other Tretrets surrounding her. This small human felt saddness and remorse at the loss of some of their own.

Davis and the Tarnet Commander were in deep conversation when Alina joined them at the Captain's table. There was a small energy drain that engineering could not account for. Davis had the lead engineer and a Sinefor team try to find the cause. What they discovered was several collectors that were not there before. They considered siphoning off the energy and removing the collectors. They also thought that if there were collectors the enemy would return for them. The enemy that stole the head from her grave were now identified. They called themselves Corian's. The Long Island had a long history of interfering with their plans and their solution was to kill her and end the problem. It was a unanimous decision of the council ship commanders to multiply the Corian's misery. Still a little unsteady on her feet she would not fall. Everytime she began to a huge arm would catch her. Engineers asked to approach the Captain's table. Alina motioned them forward. The collectors were isolated and the siphoning had been started. Duplicate collectors were put aboard battle craft with markers that would make an enemy believe the battlecraft was the Long Island. Torpedos set for remote detonation were placed in the crafts hold. When the enemy came for the collector they would find more than they wanted. Proximiy detonators were installed as a fail safe.

The Corian's thought that a charge of war crimes against Captain Grant would give the Planetary Council pause to think about things. Instead the Council and the council ship commanders laughed at the ludicrous idea of such charges. Outraged the Corian's threatened repercussions against Captain Grant and her ship. The Corian's feeling powerful from their threats met Captain Davis, the Tarnet Commander, the Volitny and Mentarran ship commanders in a hallway. They left the Council building terrified. Threats against Captain Grant dispersed into nothingness. Danielle in trying to find a causality to the events that led up to the ship being frozen looked at all the environmental conditions in the area when things happened. She marked them and set the computer to alert when the conditions matched. Staerr was monitoring the consoles and the scanners and shook her head finding nothing. Danella filled Danielle in on what occured during the time she was inactive. Even this information provided nothing useful to her that would answer why it happenned or how it bypassed all the ship's computer safety settings. Before this event intrusion alarms always stopped the attacks. The engineers and Sinefors were puzzled how it happened. The Captain was standing above the common area leaning against a bulkhead watching the lifeforms below her move about.

Danielle was trying to locate her. William was near her and told Danielle where the Captain was. She was not wanting to be disturbed unless it was critically important. Touching the comm button on her collar she answered Danielle's hail. The hallway was emptied so the Captain's passage was not hindered on her way back to the bridge. On entry she told Staerr to connect the incoming message from Captain Davis. An update on the Corian's reversal of charges was news to her. Even more so was learning that the Corian's were deeply regretful of the threats they made against her. Danielle leaned next to her and told her of the Captains meeting in the hallway with the Corian delegation. Everything fell into place once she knew that. She was smiling when she thanked the captains involved in the hallway conversation. She did not know what was discussed in that conversation though she doubted the Corian's were able to put in a single word. Staerr handed her a folded message and waited for her to give an answer. Alina told her to send back she and the ship were OK. Some small issues needed to be resolved yet. How Prime Minister Brown knew about the incident was a mystery to her.

Queen Three Sector

A LINA FELT DRAINED and mentally exhausted from all that occured. She needed some rejuvenation time. Ordering the ship to Queen Three on the pretext of getting updates on World Two Terra and World Three Atlantis the ship would pass directly over her house on World One Sam. An extended exploration of Terra was the information sent to the Planetary Council. Materializing in the front of her house she began to feel the rejuvenation of the planet already. The difficulties of command and the responsibilities were a heavy burden on her shoulders there was no doubt of that. She also knew that this is what she was meant to do with her life. Accept these burdens of command of a space ship and all the amazing life forms aboard that depended on her every day. Her Tretret guards were ever present and she could not see herself without these remarkably loyal and trusted friends about her. The presence of Corollons and Strefden around and above her, the Lomgren ever by her side and the Medusan was never far away. A new life form had been discovered while she was away on World One Sam. A giant and venemous snake over twenty one feet long. It was captured and sent to the council for examination and classification. The venom virulent even a few feet away was among the most toxic in council records.

The children in the village across the lake from her house had grown considerably while she was away. The planet was proving to be the ideal environment to raise children. Few predators and those were easily detectable by the Lomgren from a long distance off.

The planet offered considerable varities of plants, vegetables, fruits and especially tea and coffee bean harvests for the taking. She was relaxing in a chair on her front porch when the Tretret closed in on her, the Lomgren were highly agitated and the Cerollon took to the sky in large numbers. Centaurs armed themselves, Amdors retrieved hidden power weapons, William and his surface force were armed and ready to repel the unknown aggressors and the bridge had the weapons systems powered up and online for immediate use. Four battle craft descended from the overcast skies and hovered directly over the Captain. The children and families in the village across the lake were absent from her view. All rushed inside their homes at the sound of an alarm emnating from speakers all around the village. A single Corian ship was detected entering World One Sam air space and would not answer warning hails. A battle craft of a sudden shot forward in an attack posture homing in on an approaching dot in the sky.

Behind the Tretret all Alina could see was glances of an approaching ship taking hits from a battle craft and spiralling into the ground. The crew aboard the battle craft surrounded the burning ship and several went aboard the Corian ship for survivors. Six survivors were brought out and a Medusan was already in their midst looking at each survivor. When the Captain was brought forward to see the survivors she was surprised to see an Orion among the dead. Communiques from several council ships were already flooding in about the Captain and wanting to know what was going on. Was assistance needed? Messages sent back that an Orion was among the dead sent the New Iberia and the Tarnet Comand ship scrambling to her location. In an effort o detrmine every aspect of why the ship was here Amdors, Sinefors and Dofgraras were employed to decipher all communications, messages and computer system programs. Of the six survivors were delegates from the Mentarran system which raised a few questions. Locating the Captain was easy. All Davis and the Tarnet commander had to do was look for a small army of ships and a gathering of her personal guards. She would be the one in the center of all of it.

The Tarnet Commander had the Orion transported aboard his ship for removal. Council representatives already aboard the New Iberia were talking with the Mentarran delegates. Davis was becoming more and more furious at the disdain which hte Corians were regarding the Captain's presence. Amdors reported to Captain Davis that there were no weapons aboard the ship. Attack was not the reason they were there. Looking around them all the Corians could see was a wall of Tretret and gleaming edged weapons held by Strefden. No doubt for them. They were right. Cerollons flew in patrol patterns overhead. The Corians could not miss seeing them and their weapons at the ready. One tried to approach Alina and was stopped by a massive hand blocking him. Pushing it away was lost effort on his part. Ducking under it was to no avail. He was swept up by this massive hand as if he were a piece of tissue and tossed backward just as easily. A Strefden blade was near his heart, if he had one and was ready to cut him in half with the smallest effort. The Corian tried to appear menacing to the Strefden. His effort was wasted on a trained warrior and veteran of many battles. He did not see the blade move to his eyes the movement was so quick. Frozen in place the Corian was not so brave now.

The council representatives were speaking with the ships captains and it was decided the Mentarrans were free. The Corians would be taken back to the Planetary Council to be judged for their crimes. The Medusan was able to ascertain the Corians thought the Captain vulnerable on the planet and spiriting her away a simple task. Afterward they would make their demands for her return. Reprisals so long as she was in their custody was not a concern. The Mentarrans were simply a mask to their end purpose. They were convincingly told this was a diplomatic venture nothing more. The Tarnet Commander volunteered to transport the Corians to the council planet. What shape they were in on arrival was not discussed. The wreckage was transported aboard the Long Island for further examination and disassembly of all systems. All trace of the previous events were removed. Peace was restored to World One Sam. As a side note the Captain did send a team to Terra to do a planetary scan.

The Captain spent another eight days on the planet doing necessary everyday tasks and communicating with Danielle and Staerr on almost an hourly basis. Engineering was a frequent visitor during these days bringing her up to date on the ships condition. On her return to the bridge she felt renewed and almost younger than when she transported down the days before. Orders to set course for earth sector were already plotted and ready to be executed. The Lunar City would be one of her stops it always was. A message from Houston was waiting for her. They were making huge advancements in every aspect of research and sciences. They sent a thank you for her assistance in opening these doors to them. Physicians that were in Edinburgh returning to the United States were able to show vast improvements of patient care and disease control. In a year renal disease would be history. Dialysis would not be necessary. Other diseases would be very close to cures in five years or less. Genetically specific cancer cures were becoming a reality not a destination. Science was pulling the majority of the world into a cohesive group. Space travel to some nations was restricted or nonexistent. Because of the Advisor program bases and new colonies on other worlds was rapidly becoming truth not imagination.

The Constitution of the United States prohibits any person or persons not of natural American birth from holding high elective office. An advisor therefore could not hold a Congressional Representative, U. S. Senate seat or the Presidency. Other nations had already or had such changes before their legislative governing branches for consideration. Many nations were reluctant to bring such ideas to their negotiations. The United Nations, the European Union and The South East Asian Treaty Orginazation (SEATO) were not sure this was the way to go. Giving someone or thing from another world governing power over their countries and international institutions did not sit easily with them.For every disease on earth that a solution was found the possibility of a disease from another world held earth scientists from sway and being complacent. In the space sciences and other fields every answer yielded a hundred questions of what if or what is this, can we do that and the laws of physics and sciences says this can't be done then why is this like this or that?

Danielle reminded the Captain earth sector in three hours and the Lunar City would be in transport range in four hours. Deciding to take a scout ship to the surface she had one readed and a battle craft near by just in case. The Long Island would always be very near to her at a moments notice. Stepping onto the surface she walked to the wrecked lander and the body near by. A mannequin woul replace the body in the suit so it too would recieve the final honors it was due and buried with it's shipmates. All those left behind by the culture that chose to leave them like expendable nothings would now be remembered. The Prime Minister asked to be included in the burial party. Several Royal marines would be appointed pallbearers. Those that had been so before jumped at the oportunity to return to the moon. A battle craft descended from the Long Island and the Prime Minister, his personal guard and six Royal marines walked onto the moon's surface. The Marines took their place at the coffin and easily lifted it. The wonders of the universe dispalyed before them never failed to amaze them. It was not lost to any of those assembled there that the earth was above them in the sky. In a new morning the moon would be above them once more. The cemetery was growing in size. Most couuld not get over the gargantuan city next to them. The spire of the main building rose so high it's pinnacle could not be seen. The nameplate of the one being laid to rest only said "The One That Was Lost Is Now Remembered". Alina never missed the opportunity to walk to specific graves and pause at each one. William was beside her and she would tell him how she remembered all of those laid to rest here. The lifeforms that were ejected into a sun never left her memory. Those lives even if she never knew them were precious too. A disease had killed them and by ejecting all traces of the virus into the sun with them she destroyed their killer at the same time.

Population Of The Moon

THE POPULATION OF the moon is up in the air as the rocks themselves are a lifeform. Generally considered to be uninhabitable the moon is covered in rocks and rock formations hence the population of the moon could theoretically be in the billions. Appearing lifeless the rocks themselves tend to come alive in the presence of other living beings. Apollos eighteen, nineteen and twenty discovered this fact with tragic results each mission. Russian and Chinese missions to the moon suffered the same destinys. When the Captain goes to the lunar city William's team sweeps the area for recent accumulations of lunar rocks. Destroying the larger ones the smaller are thrown to distances rendering them harmless to her and the crew. Apparently androids are not preferred dining choices of the rock creatures. Being the Captain of the Long Island Alina has come to accept that the definiton of life cannot itself be defined. Rock formations vary from small groups to massive formations hundreds of mies long and dozens of miles wide. When the lunar scan satellite discovered the wreckage of the Long Island as it is now known, the image sent to Houston was of a rock formation resembling a ship.

Colonel Davis found the ship and the future of the earth and planets discovered because of his chance discovery is history. Commanding the New Iberia Captain Davis like Captain Grant are a part of something far larger than they could have ever guessed existed. Friends made that would last a lifetime and responsibilities that are staggering to bear are an everyday thing. The remnants of the early landing craft of the nations that tried to colonize the moon litter the rims of craters. The bodies of the crews that died as a result of collecting the lunar rock creatures and destroyed by them lay about their landing craft. The lack of any atmosphere on the moon has left these remains as they were when they died. William makes sure that the Captain never sees them by intentionally altering the flight path of the landing battle craft to the city and cemetery avoiding the possibility that she or her surface party see these mangled remains. Remains of other lifeforms dot the lunar landscape from times long forgotten. Victims of the rock creatures they too are evidence of a lesson learned with deadly consequences.

It is of course impossible to determine which are indeed just rocks and those that are not. Humans have a problem relating life to a rock so for now the earth says the moon is desolate of life. The Tarnet Commander thought of donating thousands of lunar rocks to the new Orion world. Life has too many variables to be catagorized into a fixed definition. Alina no longer was astonished that cats would be discussing celestial mechanics mathematics or that Centaurs would be wandering the halls of the ship valued members of the crew. Medusans were an accepted norm on the ship and no one was amazed at their presence. Shape shifters were a part of the crew as much as any other lifeform. Why couldn't rocks from a moon be alive in their own sense of existence? On World One Sam the Centaurs would do far ranging patrols and make discoveries of new animals or find unknown rivers and lakes, mountain valleys and meadows teeming with life. Finding food and water on their ranging patrols was never a problem as they were surrounded by them in vast quantities for the choosing.

For the first time larger predators were being encountered. The Cerollons had to be very alert to large avian type predators that saw them as a new meal source. A large cat was beginning to track the Captain's Tretrets. The Lomgren detected them a long way away still so the Tretrets, Amdors and the Lomgren themselves knew where they were before they were seen. Centaurs were having some difficulty detecting them so the Captain sent Lomgren with the Centaurs when they roamed. The sound of rocks moving on their own was evident and presented another possible threat to the Captain. On the moon rocks that appeared to be silicate in nature had the ability to explosively move themselves large distances or attack a prey. Crystalline stones were particularly prone to this trait. William's team was always on high alert at the lunar city watching for stones that might be missed in their scan. A rip or penetration of a suit was certain death for the hapless victim. The ship, in reality, depended on the life of the Captain for it's own existence. When the Captain was believed dead Captain Davis assumed command of the Long Island and the New Iberia so the ship and her remarkable crew did not perish.

Danielle was Alina's saving grace more than once since assuming command. When she was injured the ship was on continous alert. This last time when the ship was frozen the Captain only being unconcious saved the ship from destruction. Her death would have closed all life functions aboard the ship. So she knew the ship was tied to her. The ship was her. A wayfaring lunar stone flying at her and penetrating the suit would end her life and the ship. Shields carried by some of William's team always surrounded her on the moon. Far enough so as not to crowd her but close enough to step between her and a troubling flying rock. Everyday Danielle learned more about the Captain. This small human held more in her heart than Danielle thought could be stored. Her mind worked in ways she could not understand. This thing called imagination gave the Captain unprecented ability to see an outcome or problem before it ever occured. How humans understood something without speaking of it or when seeing someone read them as the Captain had said "like a book' or 'see right through them' and know their true nature never failed to leave questions in her processor. Humans, Danielle learned, were extremes in range. Compassion toward those she lost and compassion and caring to her crew yet be cold as empty space to an enemy. Curiosity in an unquenchable measure and denial of understanding mercy in a battle.

Being on the moon was a particular pleasure for the Captain despite the dangers present. The city held a fascination to her and the unfulfilled desire to know so much more about those who built it. How could she learn to read the volumes in tomes in the library and what secrets did they hold to a reader? Even here William's team swept the buildings for errant rocks before the Captain entered. Her life was critical to thousands of lifeforms. The Tretrets, Strefden, Lomgren and Amdors had until Captain Davis never seen much less heard of a human. They could not imagine serving under any Captain other than a human now. When they were in Sanwich, England and the Dofgrara were able to read first hand the Magna Carta did their understanding of the Captain blossom. They were currently in Queen Three a long, long way from earth sector. Alina had been thinking of the English countryside recently and always of Sherman, Texas. Wondering how her mother and family was doing. One thing had to be done first in earth sector before she could go home for a visit. The lander that carried Captain Davis was missing.

Captain Davis would investigate the matter himself. Alina didn't need to concern herself with it. As with Captain Grant's team Michael's team would sweep the immediate area of any rocks that were a threat to Captain Davis. On earth a Sidewinder rattle snake leaves a distinctive track. Tracks very similar were left by moving rocks on the moon and could be followed to their source easily enough. The larger ones were destroyed. Captain Davis had told Michhael of a game on earth called Golf. Designing a club like the Captain's description his team took turns hitting smaller rocks, silicate and crystalline stones long distances through the lunar sky. Shields stopped the flights of those explosively launched and then they were hit by the clubs. They could be hit much farther away than could be thrown so the technique worked out well. An entire group of stones began moving and all of them were destroyed. Tracks with three toes were found where the lander had been so they were dealing with sentient beings.

Home Is Never Far Away

ALINA ORDERED THE ship into geosynchronous orbit above Houston making no attempt to mask it's presence. She transported down to Sherman, Texas choosing to be put down near the street corner of her family's house. She walked the remainder of the way down the lane. The entourage with her was difficult to miss. The giant's with her stood out like strobe lights in a darkened sea. Her mother was in the front yard tending the garden and turned to see this army around a very tiny in comparison woman. Her squeal of delight was not understood by the Tretret and Alina held up her hand to stop him. The Captain was thrilled to be there that was all that mattered. Her group was drawing unwanted attention. A touch of her hand on her Tretret commanders shoulder and all were aboard the ship in a the span of a breath. Much as she wanted to be in Texas it wasn't feasible. Alina and her mothher wandered the halls of the ship with no destination in mind.Talking about everything and nothing the two spent hours just talking. Alina spoke a single phrase and on arrival to the Captain's table food for both was already waiting for them.

As her daughter had experienced before, the wonder of the lifeforms on the ship amazed her mother without end. A small creature about three feet tall pulled on her mother's arm and in tones and clicks said something to her. Danielle translated that they were happy she was aboard. Danielle said that an update on the Constellation was coming in. Alina explained that the Constellation was a ship that her ship discovered floating free in space. Apparently designed to transport an entire civilization at one time the ship was being examined in detail by the Planetary Council scientists. At the mention of the Planetary Council it was clear she had no idea what the council was. Alina said it would take time to explain. With two percent of the ship explored no signs of the culture that sent it was located. The power sections and weapons were explored first and stabilized into a station keeping mode as far as the scientists could determine. It would be years before even half the ship was explored. Her mother asked how big is this thing. "About fifteen hundred miles long and six hundred wide, more or less. That's why it's called the Constellation." "A single ship is that big? Are you kidding me?" "No, we found it adrift and the council sent research ships and a crew to pilot it back to the council planet. For the crew and culture that built it home was never far away."

Alina passed a note to Danielle who nodded she understood and holding her mother's hand both with her regulsr surface team were back in Texas ouside San Antonio. "How do you do that? I couldn't get used to that", were the first words from her mother. How long to get back to my house I wonder?" In a moment she was standing in her own front yard. "Stop that." Looking around her she could see her neighbors looking all around apparently for her. "Alina why can't they see or hear me?" "We are cloaked. My surface team tends to draw attention so we are hidden from them." "Just as well we are cloaked. See that man over there in the green shirt? He has bothered me for weeks. Even tried to hit me once." At that Alina told William to send him to section four. She would make a decision about him at a later time. As quickly as they had traveled to Sherman the man was being led to a cell aboard the Long Island in section four. His struggles were fruitless against a much stronger android. His demands of where he was fell on empty halls of the cell block. His power depended on others fearing him. Here in section four his definition of fear would gain a new personal meaning. At Alina's request the Tarnet Commander's ship took him aboard. Happy to oblige her the man would learn what Tarnet prisons were like. When he failed to show up for a court appearance a search was started and a warrant issued. During a discussion with a Tarnet advisor in Houston NASA was told the man would not be found. He was in a prison on the Tarnet home world. His crime was not specified but the Captain of the Long Island personally requested he be sent there.

Home to Alina would always be Sherman,Texas. She decided to show her mother her most secret hideaway. Setting course for Queen Three the ship arrived in two days time. Alina showed her things and new worlds that no human would ever see. Terra Two was the reality of a prehistoric world in real time. Flying in a battle craft above the dinosaurs her mother experienced wonder first hand. Life forms extinct on earth for sixty five million years paraded below her in their natural habitat. Stegasaurus, Velociraptors and Tyranosaurus were all about her. Triceratops were near by lumbering through the jungle canopy. Creatures of eneormous size and ferocity looked skyward to see this intruder above them. The pilots kept their eyes and scanners on the Pterodactyl, Pterosaurs and Pteranodons. Stunning bursts of intense light and sound kept them at bay and not a threat to those aboard the battle craft. At her order they were transported back aboard the ship. World One Sam was a few hours away. New information from World Three Atlantis shed more information on the civilizations living there and the undersea archeological wonders it concealed beneath the waves. Danielle signalled the ship was entering World One Sam orbit. The Captain and her party would be transporting down in a few minutes.

Alina materialized on the lawn in front of the house she so dearly loved. Her mother grabbed her hand not sure of the ground she was standing on. More of those amazing creatures on her ship were there. The sound of children playing was a welcome surprise to Alina's mother. A sound completely unexpected on a new planet. The realization that she was indeed standing on a new planet was incredible to even think of yet here she was. Where ever her daughter went there were those giants never far away. The Lomgren welcoming her she could not quite get used to yet. The Centaurs were everywhhere as well as those with the long bladed weapons. Shadows from above caused her mother to look skyward. The Cerollons wheeling and turning, climbing and diving in the skies was a wonderous and delightful view. Her mother understood why her daughhter loved this place. The sun had a warming feeling on her skin and the lunch prepared for them was delicious and perfectly prepared although there were some foods she wasn't quite sure of what it was supposed to be.

The tragedy of her daughters death in space was no longer in her mind. The mourning had become a fierce pride and joy when she thought of her daughter. Why she had made a complete turn around about Alina her family could not begin to understand. Home was where her daughter was, on the ship or a planet surface somewhere in a new sector of space or even the moons surface. Even here home was never far away. The fearsome power of the Long Island was always there in the back of her mind. Power that could destroy a planet at the command of her daughter's whim. Her mother sensed a father daughter pride in Alina from Captain Davis. She had warned him that if anything ever happened to her daughter he would answer to her for it and all the council ships powers would not save him. Captain Davis believed her. At her mothher's home in Sherman, Texas a rose of very unusual appearance appeared overnight. The flower was unlike any rose known by any nursery. It's size and beauty was unparalled. When asked what the rose was called she would just say it was a Captain's Rose. The county agricultural agent tried to take it and was almost hit by a shovel. "I need to take this flower and study it. I have the authority to take it if I feel it could be a danger to the State of Texas." "The only authority you have is to get your ass off my property before I shoot you. I will give you a cutting but that is all." With those words she gave him a single leaf from the flower and told him to get off her land.

Bad Feelings

ALINA AWOKE WITH an uneasy feeling in her spirit. nothing she could define in words but it was there and would not go away. Entering the bridge she asked for ships condition. Danielle said all was normal, the ship was at peak performance. Wandering to different stations she hovered around the weapons station. Danielle knew her well enough by now to know she was anxious about something. Consistently checking the weapons status was unusual for her. She had not ordered a condition three alert but clearly the Captain was upset about something. Again the Captain asked about the weapons status and wanted a very long range scan done. Alina called for status of medical bay and security status aboard the ship. The Captain would not stay seated in her chair. She would constantly look around the bridge asking if all stations were adequately manned and in readiness. Danielle assured her they were. Her Tretret Commander did not miss the Captain's nervousness and anxiety. Additional security forces were moved to the bridge. Quietly the crew assumed their battle stations. Battle craft were manned and prepared for immediate deployment.

The Dofgrara were scanning every frequency and monitor available to no avail. They could not find any sign of impending threat but the Captain's actions deepend their efforts to find if they were overlooking something. Using their private frequency Danielle advised Danella that the ship was at high combat alert. Something was wrong and the ship would remain at alert until something happened or the Captain began to calm. Her current actions gave no clue that would be any time soon. Staerr said nothing was indicated on any of the long range scans. As far as the instumentation showed there was nothing within eight million kilometers of the Long Island on any axis. Sitting in her chair Alina ordered the Long island to course two one eight on axis K. She could feel the ship change attitude and direction. The uneasiness would not diminish. Something was wrong but she could not find it on the scanners. Her lead engineer was next to her as he always was. She talked to him quietly and he left the bridge headed to the scanning control station on deck twelve.

Captain Davis was beginning to wonder about Alina when a report that the Long Island's weapons systems were fired. Danella reported that the ship had fired a full spread of torpedos at eighty one percent yield and was changing course and speed as she was speaking to him. Ordering the New Iberia to battle stations and to take an intercept course for the Long Island. Another spread of torpedos had been fired with damage to the Long Island's shields. Communication channels aboard the Long Island were filled with reports of injured and casualties. The Tarnet Commander's ship, the Mentarran ship, the Volitny Commander's ship and the Conteranan ships were closing on the Long island's position. Danella reported some ships were breaking off on an intercept course for the New Iberia at battle speeds. Davis shook his head that someone would be so stupid to attack his ship. Trying to ambush the New Iberia at battle stations? Really? The attackers would find the council's senior Captain a deadly adversary. Boarding parties from the Tarnet and Mentarran ships were ready to make the battle personal to the attacker's crews. Danella turned to Davis and said "Eleven seconds to contact Captain."

What was it about his little girl that life forms didn't like was a question Davis could not answer. Attacks against her was a direct attack on him and his crew. Shields were at maximum strength as the attacker's ships tried to overwhelm the New Iberia. A skilled battle leader Captain Davis was not a victim by any definition. The boarding parties breaching some of their ships was an unplanned contingency. They fought for many minutes eventually being overwhelmed by the council boarding crews. The dog was a particularly feared unknown by the attackers. The battles against the New Iberia and Long Island continued with the enemies numbers rapidly declining. Thinking they had an opening the enemy tried to attack the New Iberia from below.Weapon impacts from the Tarnet commander's ship ended that hope. Again they were discovering these Captains were able and cunning battle veterans. The enemy tried to board and take the Tarnet ship by surprise. When they boarded they found a battle force ready to meet them. The skirmish lasted well into an hour before they were forced to surrender to the Tarnet. Looming over all of the others the Tarnet commander walked into the middle of the combat arena. Picking up the boarding party commander by his head, lifted him with out any effort, looked him right in the eyes and in a single quick motion snapped his neck. Dropping his body into the many dead already there his eyes were a dark steel grey.

As with the human in the Tarnet's prison, these 'things' would learn what fear and suffering was. What they were and why they attacked would be coerced at the cost of every one of their lives if necessary but their identity and the reason they attacked would be revealed. Danielle advised Danella that the Captain was all right. Davis was handling his own matters. The boarding parties from the New Iberia battle craft had prisoners. Michael was there overseeing the prisioners. His security team kept the prisoners down on their faces, if that was what they were supposed to be. This life form was unlike any previously encountered. The dead would be sent to the council planet for autopsy and study of their remains. The live prisoners, some of them, would be sent to the council planet for inerrogation and intelligence gathering purposes.They were the fortunate ones. Most would not make it that far alive. None of those aboard the Volitny ship or the Tarnet ships would see the end of the day. The prisioners aboard the Mentarran and Contenaran ships would fare little better. Several of the life forms aboard the Mentarran ship were considered cannibals by human definition. They would eat well this evening.

William was overseeing his own group of prisoners. At the Captain's orders they were immediately moved to section four and placed in isolation cells. Most would arrive at the council planet for interrogation. Alina was still in a rage with the attack and in a moment of revenge let her Tretret get a little punching bag excercise with a few of them. Wanting to know about their combat skills Alina had several put in restricted combat areas with Tretrets and Strefden. Their fights would be observed and those aboard the Long Island would be able to plan counter attacks and defensive actions in case there was another encounter. Aboard one of the attacker's ships the Tarnet survey team found two Orions hidden in concealed compartments. Their discovery or fate was never mentioned in any reports to the council. Alina was not pleased with her dark side coming out. Being so cold and cruel by her own definition was not normal for her. It was no surprise to her that in a one on one with the Tretret or Strefden the prisoners were no match for either one. None of the prisoners would escape to warn their own people about the council forces. Alina could not explain her bad feelings or why they occured when they did. She knew they were usually right on and should be listened to.

A message on the Captain's secure channel was coming in and she took the message in her quarters. It was Captain Davis and the other ship commanders on a common channel. "Captain," The Tarnet Commander was saying, "did you ever think of having a peaceful day without a fight ensuing?" "I don't plan on these encounters if that is what you are asking. I don't run from them either." "Alina," Captain Davis was asking, "how did you find them? We had nothing on our scanners." She replied, "Every ship leaves an ion trail because of the engine sections. I had the engineers reprogram the scanners to detect ion trails. As it was I had a few seconds before their attack started. I lost twenty one of my crew due to the attacks when one of their weapons breached a flight hangar. We did more damage to them destroying at least three of their ships." Davis was saying," I lost three of my crew and got two of their ships when they came at me."

The other Captain's reported their losses and battle damage suffereed in the fight. The Orions found on one of the enemy vessels was never brought up. The skirmish aboard the Tarnet ship was the only instance of an enemy boarding a council ship. "My losses," Alina was telling them, "could have been greater but the ship and crew were at battle stations. Don't remember ordering condition three but everything went better than it might have." "I know Alina. Danella," Davis was saying, "told me that the ship's bridge crew were responding to how you were acting. You seemed agitated for some reason. Always checking the weapons station for readiness." Alina would return to the lunar city once more. No caskets this time but she would place name plates on the wall with the names of those whose remains would never be found. Enroute to the lunar city she was talking with Prime Minister Brown. Returning to the city one more time to honor lost dead. He offered to join her with a full contingent of Royal Marines to lay the name plates of her lost crew members on the wall by the entrance to the cemetery. She thanked him but she had been offered the same by Kennedy Space Center using United States Marines to do the sad duty. Shortly after the battle an advisor approached a contact at Kennedy and asked if U.S. Marines would be available for the assignment. They were indeed available he was told.

Marines Stand In The Gap

THERE WAS A special surprise for Alina and Davis. Tony from Houston would be among the party to honor their dead. When Tony learned both were still alive he would be the surprised one in the gathering. Staff checked the suits of the Marines, rechecked them agian and then did it again. Unfamiliar with the transport system employed by the Long Island the Marines expected a ship of some type to get them. When their suits were approved as safe the Marines began to settle into waiting to be flown to the ship. When they turned around they were aboard the Long Island and the most incredible sight was before them. There must have been hundreds of sentinet beings of every description all around them. A dog welcomed the Marines aboard and told them to board the battle craft to their left. Angels flew above them and walked around them as if all this was normal everyday events. Tall men with edged weapons were standing close around someone in the middle of a protected circle. Enormous giants moved as one when she walked. William steped forward and introduced the Captain and Prime Minister Brown to the Marine Major commanding the detail. The Marines came to attention when they knew who these persons were. Centaurs and creatures with talons and wings were nearby them. Small creatures about three feet tall were in deep conversation speaking in clicks and tones waved to them as they passed. Unsure what to do they remained at attention.

A giant the size of a bear was in front of them and filling them in on what they would see and experience when they stepped out onto the moon surface. The Prime Minister was taking all of this in stride as if he had done it before. An honor ceremony would be conducted first and then they would put the name plates on the wall one at a time. Do not let their surroundings take their attention from their task. The Captain expected them to complete their task flawlessly. It was difficult not to look around them as different ships would hover or land nearby and then members of their crews would walk to the Captains and what appeared to be say they were sorry for their losses. They too had their own dead to lay to rest. Captains Grant and Davis would perform the honor ceremony for their crew members and then watch as they were laid in graves at the base of the crater. As they were leaving the Major was studying the city itself and turning one last time to those laid to rest saw the sign at the entrance of the cemetery and understood why this place was never 'found' on any scans.

When the marines were back on board the Long Island the Captain came to the Major and asked if he and his Marines could do one more thing for her. Not knowing she herself was formerly a Marine he was not sure why she was making a request of him. There was a hostage situation on the planet of Tilara. Two of the Planetary Council's ambassadors were being held hostage by a band of rebels and since the Long Island could not involve itself in the situation she was asking if his Marines could intervene for her. The planet had a one half earth gravity that might make things difficult for he and his Marines. The rebels were of a race named Corians. A briefing on them and their combat tactics would be given them. A crash course on extraterrestrial fighting would have to be learned in about four earth days time. Weapons training would be included so that they could use weapons used thousands of millenia ago on other worlds. But weapons thousands of years ahead of those on earth. The task was daunting without a doubt but it was up to the Marines to rescue the ambassadors. No other council member could be part of the effort because of interplanetary agreements.

It was because of these agreements the rebels had a sense of impunity. The Marines were a force never previously encountered or known to them. Their skills as Marines would have to carry them through the battle. Stepping onto the surface of Tilara was an experience that they would never be able to speak of. At half the gravity their jumps carried them much farther than they were used to. The weight of things on the surface were half as heavy so the effort to carry them was much less. Exertion was significantly less. The rebels would be accustomed to the gravity difference and that gave the Marines a distinct combat advantage. Half the effort was needed to accomplish the same task on earth. Feeling immune to attack the rebel patrols were not paying much attention to what was around them. One by one the rebels numbers grew smaller. The Marines had entered the outer fenced area and were now in the enemies midst. Movements would have to be more cautious. An alarm would would destroy their entire plan. A rebel happened on to a Marine patrol and not knowing who or what they were his hesitation caused him his life. Thrown into the wall his neck was thrust backward onto his spine.

The chance encounter reminded the Marines they were not in Kansas anymore and if they died here no one would know what truly happened to them. Moving forward cautiously they were brought to a halt suddenly by a noise ahead of them. Two rebels were on a collision course with them. More of a train derailment is what it would end up being for them when the Marines attacked by surprise. Silent and very quick the rebels deaths were no challenge at all for them. False confidence was a potential killer. Staying close to the building the Marines moved forward cautiously. A door on the left slid open almost silently as several rebels walked out directly into the Marine patrol. Knives flashed in the waning Tilaran sun and the dead never knew what happened. Inside the hallway split into three hallways. The briefing before they landed on the planet told them where they needed to go and whom to expect from the other two halls. Charging forward down the adjacent halls the Marines met their enemy before they could plan a defense. The third hall would take them to a room where the ambassadors would be. The strongest resistance would be here. When the first alarm did sound the Marines were already at the rebels center of operations.

Before the rebels could kill the ambassadors the Marines blew the door open and charged in force inside. Fierce hand to hand fighting lasted for many minutes. The rebels could not identify these attackers. They certainly did not fight like any member of the council. Their strength was greater than any force they had encountered before. Their fighting technique was unknown to them and intimidation was useless. A rebel tried to grasp a Marine from behind and was tossed over his head with very little effort. Slammed into the floor he was stunned and unable to fight. The ambassadors were swept up and rushed down the hall. Rebels trying to impede them were moved aside like children. As soon as they were back outside the Marines and ambassadors were transported aboard the New Iberia. The Corian ambassadors were already complaining about the raid which Captain Davis said never occured. Again feeling powerful with their position they remained so until they realized they were on an unknown planet alone. The ambasadors returned to their home worlds the Marines prepared to return to theirs. In the forward confrence room space was shown in it's greatest splendor as they marvelled at hings no human may ever see again. Galaxies, star clusters, black holes and stars being born and dying were there for them to see. The ship would change course to allow them to see new worlds the council would soon explore but had not gotten around to yet. Creatures on these planets that none could describe lumbered over mountains and vales, some flew through gas clouds with out harm a human could not survive a minute in. The seas of these worlds held wonders like hundred foot long sharks and fish that had never seen man before and never would.

It was with reluctance to many that it was announced the earth sector was close. They would be home after the debriefings. Seeing and fighting on another world, burying remains of another civilization on the moon and seeing the wonders of space within a few light years of earth. Not even a thumbnail layer of skin to what is out there. They did remember passing by the warning posts of dark space. The emptiness and unending nothingness it was. As astonishing as all these things were it did not compare to being able to sit down and talk to the amazing crew of this ship. Who would have thought a Marine would be speaking to a Centaur or Tretret or Strefden about fighting. The Lomgren held most of the Marines fascinations. Walking through the ship's hallways having to move to avoid hitting a lifeform walking past them on the cieling was an experience none would forget. The Marines never gave a second thought to standing shoulder to shoulder with any fighting force on earth. Even the tallest of them stood shoulder to hip with some of the life forms on the New Iberia. The Tarnet crews had respect for the Marines that fought those few days ago on a new world against an unknown and unearthly enemy. Earth was a ship's time period away. The Marines would be set down one mile from their base gate. Assembled on the flight deck the Major turned around to say goodbye to Captain Davis and the familiar smells of the sea filled his nostrils. The sun was high in the sky and storm clouds were gathering in the northwest.

The Marines had been to the moon, forced their way aboard an alien space craft and fought on a planet far from earth against an enemy that humans didn't know existed. Made friends with, trained side by side with life forms from planets and systerms light years away and moved through space and distances in a moments span of time. And no one could ever know anything about what they did..ever.

The Marines saw regions of space and things that took their breath away with the stark beauty and sometimes violent natures displayed. Ships passed near them that the crew of the New Iberia took no special notice of. Danella was an amazing lady. She was beautiful and intelligent and always accompanied by four giants very close by. A life form, well known to the New Iberia as a problem where ever encountered, forced a boarding to stop an attack on the New Iberia. It was no surprise to Captain Davis the boarding was a rough one. Weapons fire was unwise in a confined ship so the Marines engaged the Tanrians in hand to extremity combat. Lomgren were ferocious in the fighting and despite injuries to themselves kept attacking with deadly preciseness. The skirmish was long and brutal because of the type of combat. The Marine's knives were used instead of their weapons. Captain Davis allowed weapons used in the Marine's combat encounters to return with them. Trophies that did not exist according to the Marine Corps. No parades or medals for what they did. The Department of the Navy said the Marines were part of a secret multinational training excercise somewhere in Asia.

An Old Friend Comes Aboard

TONY WAS THINKING of his experience on the moon's surface as he had almost constantly since returning. There was something about the Captain's of the Long Island and New Iberia. It was almost as if he was intimately familiar with them but he couldn't put his finger on exactly why he felt so. His cancer was cured despite all medical reasoning. The three DNA genes that didn't exist before were almost certainly responsible for his healthiness now. Where they came from and why then in time was still a mystery to him. Images of Colonel Davis and his Alina with angels near them seemed to be the turning point of his cancers remission. He thought it ironic that life should return to him when death's precipice was imminent. Houston was monitoring the International Space Station's progress when the Long Island, making no attempt at concealment, apeared on their scanners in orbit above the city. In the night sky her length and size was easy to see with the naked eye. Micah, the android that contacted them before, was calling the Space Center on an open channel. News channels were already broadcasting the Long Island in clear view from the ground. Tony was giving a public relations talk to the media when the ship appeared overhead.

Even more captivating to the news stations was the descent of the Captain's yacht as it neared the Space Center. It stopped and hovered silently five hundred feet off the tarmac. For such a massive craft her quietness was a surprise. As always the security landing team exited first. Creatures of such amazing wonder to the news reporters and crowd gathered there enhanced all the more by the inclusion of Centaurs in the team. For some reason there was an absolute fascination with the Centaurs more so than the others. Then the cameras shot skyward as the Captain, her beauty radiant in the evening light, descended from the ship alighting gently on the tarmac. Four massive creatures closed around her immediately as a formidable shield. A Strefdan walked over to Tony and pulled him forward toward the Captain. Placing her hand on his shoulder they began to rise together to the ship awaiting them. As quickly as the landing party had arrived they disappeared from the reporters cameras. The yacht began to tilt upward and in a few moments was lost to sight. Danielle was waiting for the Captain's return and had an honor guard specifically to greet Tony aboard.

Alina disembarked and Danielle said that the Captain would send for him later at the Captain's table. In the meantime there were things the Captain wanted him to see. More of these massive creatures were all about and creatures he could not begin to imagine in his mind were in the hallways. Lomgren welcomed him aboard and creatures that looked like Medusa were nearby. Cerollon called to welcome him and he looked around for them until Danielle indicated he look up. There were creatures the stuff of science fiction horror movies yet they were proving intelligent and friendly willing to engage him in conversation at every turn. There were individuals following them and Tony asked Danielle about them. They are with the medical bay in case he had any trouble with the diversity of life and shock should set in. So far things were fine he was just startled at the lifeforms in one place. Danielle pointed out what looked like cats on their hind legs. Danielle told him they were part of engineering specifically handling complex engineering calculations and biochemistry equations. As Danielle pointed and told him about specific life forms Tony's mind was having trouble processing some of it. The medics were beside him before he could fall. He didn't remember going down any hallways but he was on a table in the medical bay looking up at the Captain. He knew her, he was sure he knew her. Colonel Davis was there too beside her. The Captain said to him "Tony remember when you told me if anyone could beat this I could?"

Recognition hit him like a a sea wave. Alina. His Alina was the Captain of this ship. And Colonel Davis? Alina said that Davis was the Captain of the ship New Iberia. Slowly things were falling into place and understanding was opening his eyes to truth. Captain Davis's home town was New Iberia, Louisiana hence his ship's name. Neither Alina or Davis were dead. They commanded ships of enormous size and diversity of lifeforms. Davis explained that their ships were part of an interplanetary organization called the Planetary Council. There were more than three hundred fifty members of the Council comprising planets and planetary systems spanning several galaxies. Medics helped Tony sit up slowly and then watched him for any sign of recurrance. Captain Davis held his hand out to Tony who quickly took it and smiled at seeing his old friend again. By the way some of their best friends in the Council will be joining them for dinner. "You will stay for dinner won't you?" Alina was asking. "Absolutely I will stay, be my pleasure", was out of his mouth before he could think it. Danielle said that at a later time she would brief him on some of the bad guys out there that earth may encounter at some point. Their strengths and weaknesses and the dangers to humans who contact them unprotected without isolation suits.

As they entered the dining area food for the others were being brought out as well. Tony was positive he did not want to even guess what some of these things were he was seeing. That looked like live scorpions and extra large tarantulas and what ever that was that stunk horribly was being devoured by one of the lifeforms like it was a delicacy. The dinner brought to them was a steak cooked just to his preference with all the sides, dessert and iced tea with a touch of medicinal Scotch. Alina said that she got the steaks the last time she was on earth. Tony was about to ask her about that comment when several life forms walked into the Captain's dinig area. One was almost three meters tall with reddish gold hair and eyes like clear crystalline glass. Others that were there would prove more difficult for him to describe. Before the evening was over they were talking like old friends. The different species was becoming easy to accept and he no longer understood his difficulty with them when he was brought aboard. Danielle walked up to the Captain and Alina rose quickly her guard on her heels. When they entered the hallway an alarm was sounding and the other Captains disappeared one by one. Tony was led to the bridge and told to stay in the background. Alina was in her chair and the chaos on the bridge he began to realize was a practiced response to a battle alert.

A bridge officer Alina addressed as Staerr was giving her the ship's condition battle readiness. Creatures he had not seen before Alina called Dofgrara were busy monitoring a communications station and interpreting languages Tony could not recognize. He felt the aspect of the ship change and the speed increase was only evident on the main screen image as planets and stars fell behind them rapidly. A tactical display on a side screen showed the position of the other Captain's ships in relation to the Long Island. Danielle said that the Long Island's position was always in the center of the display.

Danielle pointed out the New Iberia, the Volitny, Bolterer Cantarraian and the Tarnet Command ships on the tactical display. Sixty one degrees either side of this group were additional Planetary Council ships. Their combined weaponary power would prove overwhelming to any force Tony could concieve of existing. Those responsible for the disabling of the Long Island were fleeing when they detected the council ships force in pursuit of them. Space opened in a kaleodoscopic window of light and they were gone. A long distance scan showed no ships other than the council vessels inside an eight million kilometer distance. After a few minutes the ship stood down from combat alert. Tony saw in Alina during this event something in her he had not noticed before. It was if Alina disappeared and the Captain took over. It was also obvious that she belonged in that chair. Overlapping communications sounded like gibberish to him but the Dofgrara were not having any problem disseminating these calls.

What Tony did not and could not understand is how and why the ship and her crew were dependent on her for their existence. Her every move was followed by the bridge crew and their respect for her as Captain was apparent. The man she called William was always near her as were these giants that dwarfed any normal sized man on earth. She was talking with Danielle and a simple glance from her had Tony moved backward out of hearing range. Staerr and William were in that conversation group and at it's conclusion things began to move quickly. A whispered message to the Centaur on the bridge and he too left the bridge to carry out his task. The Tretret commander moved additional security onto the bridge. Alina left the bridge with Tony encouraged by William to follow her to the transport pad on deck eight. A member of the Council was arriving and the Captain greeted him. The woman he knew as Alina, as Tony had seen before, was gone and the Captain was with out question in complete command. Captain Davis and the Tarnet Commander materialized along side him and the four left togther. Alina did introduce Tony to the Council representative who wanted to talk to him specifically. What Tony could offer him was a mystery. The conversation between them would for Tony no doubt prove ground breaking.

It was much later in the ship's time periods that the Representative came to his quarters. At the Captain's orders the quarters were sealed. Tony alone could break the seal at his command. The representative spoke of

an opportunity that floored Tony. Be the Council delegate on earth with
the possibility of his own command later. The ship would not be as large
as the Long Island or the New Iberia but it was a new one only a year old
since launch. In the meantime he would recieve information that in his
wildest imaginings could he have contemplated as true. When Tony did
break the seal did he learn of a secret held by the Captain, her most treasured
place of places and they were going there now in Queen Three. World One
Sam grew larger and larger on the ship's screen. Before they arrived there
Alina showed him World Two Terra and World Three Atlantis. He was
stunned that worlds like these existed and yet here they were. The Tarnet
Commander told him that all three planets were the Captain's. She had
claimed them and the Council had approved her claims consequently there
were protectd by Council law. Council research teams were the only off
worlders allowed on them.

World One Sam was the planetary image of paradise that Tony could
have envisioned. No wonder Alina loved being here. There was sometihng
about this place that just made him feel good, better than he had in a long
time. He was sitting on the patio with the Captain discussing the other
two planets. The catastrophic events that would happen if even one of the
animals on Terra was released on earth was too much to think of. The
sound of children playing across the lake was a welcome surprise. There
was a peace here that reached deep inside him. No where on earth did
he have this feeling and he did not want to leave. Alina asked him if the
Council representative mentioned getting his own command. He had
and was not sure he had what it took to hold such a responsibility. What
puzzled him was why he was chosen as a candidate for command. Alina
said "Because Captain Davis and I recommended you." He would accept
the offer of Council delegate and wanted to know more about the ship that
could be his. Alina and Davis smiled at this. This curiousity was the Tony
they remembered. The ship's name would be designated as he determined.
Seven miles long and fully three miles wide with twenty one decks it was
smaller than the Long Island or New Iberia but it could be his ship.With a
crew over thirteen thousand comprising now four hundred eighty sentinent
species it was staggering to even contemplate.

Captain Davis transported him aboard the New Iberia and set course for
the Planetary Council home world. As they approached Tony saw the most

incredible thing he had ever seen. A ship of enormous size in orbit above the planet. This thing was gargantuan in scope. It was found adrift in space by Captain Grant who named it The Constellation. Council researchers believed it was intended to transport their entire civilization at one time but so far there was no trace of who or what built it. After six months less than ten percent of the ship had been explored by any measure of completion. Accessing what they believed was the crew areas was proving difficult. Entering through the hull was not an option. If any of the crew had survived breaching the hull and breaking life support was too risky. Maintaining the ship's integrity was paramount. A woman came up to Tony that he thought was Danella. "Captain, I am Carin, your second in command. The ship is waiting for you just off the port beam. This is Brian, he is your chief of security. These are your personal guard, indicating several Tretrets near them, where you go they go." Entering his bridge for the first time Tony stood and looked around. His bridge crew was standing waiting his first orders. The chair seemed to fit him perfectly. His role as delegate was mainly a ceremonial one. His real duty was as Captain of this amazing vessel.

Carin showed him the ship's layout and where specific life forms were located on the ship. He was given a tour of the engineering, maneuvering, star navigation and the medical bay and told of it's capabilities. The weapons section was the most revealing of the ship's true abilities. This firepower and the responsibility it brought with it was sobering. His ship by itself could turn a planetoid like the moon into ash in a few seconds. The most anticipated tour for Tony was that of his Captain's yacht. No where near the size of Alina's or Captain Davis's it was still an impressive craft. He saw a number of smaller craft in the aft section of the bay and was told these were his battle craft. Carin was given access to the private channel that Danielle and Danella shared. There was much to learn about a human Captain. No doubt many of his actions would surprise her, but as they had already learned, a human Captain was the most intriguing to serve under.

Human imagination allowed the Captain to plan for and see the possibilities of events before any evidence of them was apparent. Tony had much to learn about being a Captain but the other Captain's would teach him on the job. Alina told him that the first thing he needed to do was to see how his crew worked together at battle stations. Finding problems should be done now. In battle there won't be a second chance. He named the ship the Illinois Lincoln. In Staerr's position on his ship was a beautiful and charming android he named Loreena. Carin informed him that earth sector was already programmed into the navigation computer and was waiting his command. Earth. He had not thought of earth in long time. His new world would have to begin on earth. That he was leaving his old life behind was not a consideration. His entire world was now this ship and her crew. The Planetary Council and the four hundred eighty members he was now a part of concerned him. He was surprised how quickly the Captain in him had taken over. Tony was pretty much gone and the Captain and his ship was left. His family on earth would always be there. His new family was in the here and now. Warned of the possible effects of his first space jump he had medics standing by just in case. Swinging his chair to look directly at Carin he ordered the ship to head for earth sector, jump capability was authorized. "Course set for earth sector, going to jump cability Captain" was her response. "Will be entering earth sector in five ship periods."

Tony wondered if Davis and Alina felt like this when they took command. It was the most terrifying yet exhilerating feeling at the same time. Remembering Alina's suggestion he had Carin set Condition three alert to see how the crew responded. Chaos seemed to erupt until he recognized the same activity on the Long Island earlier. The crew knew their responsibilites and jobs. Loreena reported the ship at battle stations and there were three battle craft manned and ready to deploy at his command. Weapons were online and at his command. Tony saw that there was four times the number of security personnel on the bridge than normal. Brian told him that was standard procedure during an alert. The Captain's life was of absolute importance and all efforts to protect him would be employed. He had Lorenea and Carin go to each bridge station and check for problems that needed to be corrected now. An issue with a console was found and several creatures about three feet tall came onto the bridge. They were testing systems and looking for the problems in the console. The clicks and tones were a little odd at first but Carin would translate for him what they were saying. He ordered standdown from alert. He found out what he wanted for now. The Sinefor worked for three ship periods finally getting the system back into normal operation. A giant the size of a Grizzly bear standing up came onto the bridge and Carin introduced him to the Amdor engineering section commander.

"Captain", Loreena was saying, "earth sector in half a ship period." Before he could say anything Carin was ordering the ship to prepare for geosynchronous orbit over Houston. She explained about the composition of the landing party and their order of exit from the Captain's yacht. The Cerollons were first flying patterns over and around the landing area. The Lomgren were next because of their intelligence, highly developed sense of smell and extrodinary hearing. The Strefdan were next forming a wall where the Captain would be and then the Tretret that would always accompany him. Centaurs and a Medusan were always included in the landing party on the Long Island and New Iberia. Tony gave orders that they would also be included in his landing party detail. Council adivors around the globe had been advised of the new Captain and of the Illinois Lincoln. Reports were his name was Captain Tony Williams. Previously with NASA in the astronaut mission section. There was to be a welcome dinner for Tony as the newest Captain of the fleet later that evening. His ship was impressive in size and the diversity of life forms was unparalled to his knowledge on any of the other ships.

Brian had his quarters scanned by a shape shifter to detect any others that may be hidden there. Then his beverage collection was checked for any that would prove dangerous or deadly to him and removed. Finally the Captain's quarters were searched for any spiders, snakes, venomous lifeforms and scorpions hidden in the darkness of corners. Tony realized this obviously was done from experience. Brian came up to him and said there was a problem, actually five of them in section four on deck three. Walking into the prison section five creatures he was not familiar with were pacing up and down their cells. Lomgren on patrol found them nearing deck one and the bridge. No matter how they were altered in appearance the Lomgren knew the smell of an Orion and a Sorian a mile off. At his dinner he mentioned that there were three prisoners in section four that he was told were Orions. There were also two Sorians being held there. The Tarnet Commander and Volitny Captain's attention were suddenly locked onto the conversation. All conversation at the Captain's table stopped as they looked at him actively listening to what he said.

The sudden silence at the table made Tony pause. The Tarnet Commander wanted the Orions. He would be happy to take them off the Captain's hands. The Captain of the Volitny ship said the Sorians were a particular interest to his government and would take them to his ship. A nod of agreement from Alina and Captain Davis sealed the five prisoners fates. The Orions were transported from section four transport pad to the Tarnet command ship and the Sorians would disappear into the freezing penal farm on the Volitny home world. In a whispered conversation with Captain Grant she was advised the human she requested be sent to a Tarnet prison died in his cell. His hair, though he was in his early twenties, was pure white and his eyes reflected the terror that killed him. Alina thought it would be fitting to have his body discovered on a highway not far from Sherman, Texas. A wanted felon dead lying alone on a lightly travelled road in the desert.Just when things seemed to be calming down and returning to normal this body is found. A guarded conversation between the three human Captains reulted in a paln to introduce the Illinois Lincoln to the world in a spectacular way. Cloaked to hide from the earths scanners and the international space station crew the three ships assumed an orbit above London. The choice of London was due in no small part to Alina's fondness for Prime Minister Brown.

A communique materialized on his desk telling him not to get excited. There were three Council ships in orbit over London, cloaked for the moment, waiting for the right time to reveal the newest of the council ships the Illinois Lincoln. He would actually determine when that reveal happened. As it so happened the Prime Minister was to give an address to the natiion that evening. It gave him no small measure of satisfaction that he alone knew of this upcoming event. It would occur during his address according to a cue he would arrange with the Captains monitoring the address. On his cue all three Captain's yachts would descend from the darkend cloud filled sky at the same time. The wonderous creatures that would exit first and then the three Captains would descend from their ships simultaneously. The Prime Minister notified the advisors under his departments security of the impending arrivals and where it would be. The public, unaware of the event, were surprised to see advisors from all the planets of the Council in full ceremonial dress. The Royal family demanded to know why the advisors were so regalled. This speech was supposed to be just a State of the Nation and Commonwealth.

The Prime Minister assured them that this speech was indeed as intended. There would be guests arriving for the address not on the guest list. The media thinking this was just another speech were in for a long evening. The advisors were more than willing to talk to the media and the presence of Centaurs on the periphery where they were not a moment before caused a stir of excitement. People were pointing skyward as cameras swung to follow them and Cerollons were flying high above them. Several news reporters were trying for the best position to report from and were told by dogs at their feet to watch where they walked. Men that were very tall and muscular carrying large edged weapons moved among the crowd. Finally the gathering mass of people could not miss the presence of enormous creatures in front and among them. Medusans that appeared from nowhere caused many to recoil in horror at their visage. To add to this confusion men almost three meters tall walked among the crowd looking everywhere for any threat. Cats walking upright would scratch anyone that almost stepped on them warning them to look down before they crowded forward to see.

Prime Minister Brown was about twenty minutes into his address when he said that the Council had a new ship and a new Captain. In fact the individuals among them were from his ship the Illinois Lincoln. At that moment three large vessels descended below the clouds and three Captains descended slowly from their yachts to touch softly on the podium next to the Prime Minister. Appearing not to notice the Prime Minister continued his address. At it's end he turned to the Captains and welcomed them to England. The Royal family, furious they were not part of this, were about to say something when the Prime Minister invited them forward to meet the Captains and their seconds in command. Telling Danielle apart from Danella or Carin was impossible. They were identical in every manner. The only way was to see which Captain they stood with. The same was to be said of William, Michael and Brian, they too were identical in all respects.

Unexpected Revelations

MESSAGES ARRIVED FROM the Council that the civilization that built the Constellation had been found. Their remains specifically had been found. They were almost indistinguishable from the ship itself. Tests confirmed that for what ever reason the ship went into a core jump. Why a massive ship with quite possibly close to a million individuals aboard would go to a core jump was a mystery they may never solve. Speculations as to what enemy or enemies would cause them to commit mass genocide of their culture could not be guessed at. The researchers, in enviromental isolation suits, took samples of the air aboard from different sections of the ship, tissue samples when they could be found and what appeared to be a food substance were all collected and analyzed. Since the possibility of a viral infection was always a factor in their minds all testing was done under quarantine conditions. Identifiable microscopic forms were located in every quadrant of the ship. None of them were considered lethal or infectious in nature. Radiation levels were well below those considered dangerous.

Amdor engineers and Sinefors working in the engine sections discovered that the ship was capable of junp speeds plus factor of five. Technology of this scale was unknown anywhere among the Council members. More surprises awaited the engineers working to decrypt the computers aboard the Constellation. They regularly travelled across dark space regions by being able to navigate through them. Engineering teams in the weapons sections were at a loss to make any sense of them or how they operated. As expected by Captain Grant the council requested some of her engineers to help out. Engineers, the cats and Sinefors were all recruited. Only twenty volunteers were selected for the mission. The length of the task ahead of them would mean permanent reassignment to the Planetary Council staff. It also opened up twenty slots for the Long Island crew. Over four hundred applications for those slots arrived within two days time. After eighteen days of sorting and trimming the twenty slots were filled. Alina knew the Long Island was a highly desired ship assignment.

While the New Iberia and Illinois Lincoln left earth orbit the next sunrise, Alina decided to spend some time on earth and get to know England a little better. A visit to Kensington Palace was on the schedule. A schedule change demanded by the Queen herself. Alina might be the Captain of the Long Island but refusing a royal command was considered an insult to the Queen. The Royal Guard tried to seperate Alina from her security team unsuccessfully resulting in numerous casualties and injuries. None to Alina's team. Two were killed by Lomgren bites, another was beheaded and six were hit by Tretrets sending them through palace walls. Foolishly they thought surrounding them would be the end of it. The Captain and her team were there one moment and in a span of a breath back aboard the Long Island. Alina's fury at the betrayal was evident in her behavior as she fought to calm down. Repeated messages from Prime Minister Brown went unanswered. The Long Island left earth orbit flying so close to the Intrernational Space Station the ship almost hit it when it passed.

The consequences of the betrayal were evident almost immediately. Advisors became isolated and classes scheduled by them were cancelled indefinetly until the Captain of the Long Island said enough was enough. Alina ordered the Long Island to the Planetary Council planet. The Constellation would help her get through the betrayal and soothe her anger. When Alina would not respond to his messages the Prime Minister sent messages to the New Iberia explaining the betrayal by Kensington Palace. Davis could imagine Alina in a rage fueled fury at the betrayal. Davis ordered that limited contact with England would be enforced until he cleared it once more. A letter materialized on the Prime Ministers desk on Ten Downing Street. The contents, difficult for him to read, outlined the new agreement set forth by the Planetary Council regarding continuing contact with England. Severe penalties were invoked for the betrayal and attempted capture of Captain Grant. He had seen the weapons on the Long Island in action. England was a minute nuisance if the Captain chose to be truly aggressive.

As Captain of the Illinois Lincoln, Tony was discovering entirely new parameters as to what was normal now, as opposed to even a few weeks before. Planetary distress calls from worlds he had never even heard of were calling his ship by name in their communiques for assistance. Reports from the investigators on Terra and Atlantis were uncovering artifacts and ruins that had mysterious similarities to early earth history. The chair, as he called it, was a perfect fit for him. Not in regard to the size or contours but the responsibilities. Carin kept him up to date on any changes in ships status or situation awareness within the ship's area. As he walked to the Captain's table that evening he barely thought of his life before on earth. As Alina and Captain Davis had already learned the command of a ship changed every aspect of who they were as a person and how they were percieved by others. The presence of hulking giants and a small army of android security at his command where ever he went was a given.

Alina did not wake at her normal time. Without hesitation Danielle ordered her emrgency transported to medical bay and for the chief physician to stand by. It was well into the third hour of her being in medical bay before she began to stir, confused and lost, it took her a few moments to realize where she was. Her Tretret guard were inches from her side and the Strefden, Lomgren and William's security force formed an inpenetrable wall around her bed. Danielle had advised Danella and Carin of the incident but stated was not a dangerous issue and the Captains did not need to be advised just yet. Danella knowing Captain Davis chose to advise him of the problem on the Long Island. The hours before Alina revived were agonizing to him not knowing anything of what happened or why his Alina was in the medical bay. He was too far away to get to her so all he could do was wait. She was exhausted and had been pushing herself very hard and her body finally forced her to slow down and rest. Like the New Iberia all the other council ships were too far from the Long Island to go to her aid. When Alina did enter the bridge the view screen showed the Constellation and dozens of research vessels flying about it like mosquitos. She needed a recharge. Turning to Danielle she ordered the ship to Queen Three and World One Sam at best speed. Immediately Staerr had the coordinates entered and helm was preparing for jump capability. It occured to Alina with the way the the crew of the Constellation was discovered if they tried a core jump to travel faster risking their own destruction. Even for the army of Dofgrara working to decrypt and translate the Constellation's computers it would take weeks or months to find any answers.

Rest And Relaxation Or Else

THE CHIEF PHYSICIAN ordered the Captain into an eight day rest period on World One Sam. It's rejuvenating effects were lost on all but humans. The tone in her house went off and Staerr went to the communication console to check it. The Illinois Lincoln was three ship periods from orbit above the planet. She went back out to tell the Captain's Tretret guard it was the Lincoln coming into the planets region. Captain wanted to know how she was doing and if there was anything he or his ship could do for her. The problem with being the only girl Captain, as Alina saw it, was that all the other Captain's treated her like a baby sister. She was far from defenseless or need of smothering. Danielle used the time in orbit for fine tuning the instruments and navigation systems, upgrading the weapons and shields on the ship and cleaning the ship up in general. Tony had a surprise for her when he tansported down. A bundle of Sunflowers and Geraniums from Florida. Preserved aboard the ship he presented them to her just as she was going to chew him out for being overprotective. The Cerollon were looking at them hungrily and he told them they were for the Captain not their dinner. A dinner of scorpions and geraniums with a side of sunflowers just didn't appeal to Tony. Her surprise at recieving them was evident. Her eyes opened wide and she had a laugh of pure delight. She kept wanting to take some earth flowers here but always seemed to forget at the last moment.

Evening on Sam was beginning and a chill was coming on so they went inside to relax by a fireplace. This was the house Alina always dreamed of having. Problem was it wasn't in Texas. Staerr told her the New Iberia and the Tarnet Command ship were four ship periods away from the planet. Well they would just have to wait until morning because she was going to bed early. She intended to stay up quite late but being Captain did have it's perogatives and perks. Neither Captain would transport down until morning. Incurring her wrath was something both knew quite well. Respect, they told themselves, over rode valor. By mornings light the geraniums and sunflowers had been planted on the west side of the house because it got the most sun in the daytime. The smell of coffee, bacon, toast, hash browns from an indigenous relative of the potato and an egg seven inches across greeted the two captains on their arrival. Matching plates were placed before them as they sat down. The Tarnet Commander wasn't sure why he was suddenly so hungry. This food was completely unknown to him but he wasted no time cleaning the plate. These humans were always coming up with something new and different. In honor of her guests she had small four ounce steaks cooked and placed next to their plates. Tony and Davis could not eat the steaks but the Tarnet Commander did not let them go to waste. He did not know what steaks were but they were tasty.

Three days into her forced rest period Alina was feeling much better. Her skin tone was better, she had more energy and her thinking was faster and clearer. Wonderful place World One Sam. Captain Davis had no idea what he was doing when he showed this planet to a naieve Marine Lieutenant Colonel. Seemed like a lifetime ago that happened. Five more days and she was back on the Long Island. She could not wait for these five days to pass. Her family was on that ship and she was ready to go back but the physician said no wait the five days. When they had finally passed and she walked onto the bridge for the first time in eight days the sounds and sights around her were welcome indeed. Danielle briefed her on what had happened in the time she was recovering. The Constellation would retain the name she gave it but deciding on a mission for it was another matter entirely. The computers still had not been decrypted and the engines baffled every council planet members best scientists and engineers. The bridge was an enigma that could not be discerned with any clarity of functioning and operation. The language was proving the most difficult to trasnslate of any so far encountered. As a side comment Alina said try the Summarian or Egyptian languages as a key. In fact once they were compared the translations started coming quickly.

Still the picture language was a problem. Alina told the Dofgrara that in the earth's past the Aztec, Inca and Egyptian's all had picture languages, the Egyptian's was called Heiroglyphics. The similarities were astonishing and provided the needed clues to finish the translation process. What that said to Alina was that at some point in time those three cultures left earth for space. That, no matter how she thought about it, made any sense to her as to how or who took them from the surface before flying ships existed on earth. But then she thought on the Long Island itself and it's amazing crew and the advance technology it held. Anything was possible in the universe. The Illinois Lincoln was much larger and more powerful than any aircraft carrier on earth but dwarfed in size compared to the New Iberia and the Long Island was larger still. Other than size what set the Lincoln apart from other council ships was that it carried four hundred eighty sentient life forms. Most of the other ships had three hundred something or less aboard. Tony called Carin over to him and whispered something to her. In a matter of minutes two battle craft departed the Lincoln and closed on wreckage of some type near by. The computer recognized the ship as a possible virus carrier and the battle craft fired simultaneously destroying it completely.

The Long Island was passing one of the dark space perimeter warning buoys on it's way back to earth sector. There was an issue that had to be resolved one way or the other and Prime Minister Brown would have to take the brunt of her anger that still lingered even now. The crew, prepared for war if necessary, awaited the Captain's orders. Entering earth orbit cloaked she waited for a full earth day before contacting the Prime Minister. Continual communicatios between all three second's in command kept them acutely aware of events that were happening in real time. On her command a false image of the Long island appeared above the Falkland Islands. The British, Argentinian and Chilean forces went to high alert the moment it showed up on their scanners. The Captain had the information she wanted and had the image dissolved. Peace was not an option on the table right now. Fine, then the Captain had another option ready to implement. A warning letter to the Prime Minister materialized on his chief assistant's desk and rushed into his office. Transmitting on a closed channel to the ship Captain Grant responded and her demeanor was not encouraging.

The Crown would not apologize for it's actions. The Queen had her requirements that was law. World leaders saw her in private without security forces in attendance. What made Alina so special as to violate that trust? Alina had her requirements of civiilty that Kensington had violated and they too were law. She reminded him that the Queen's requirements were her's alone. Alina's requirements were based on Interplanetary laws of agreement of conduct. A Captain never went anywhere at any time without his or her security team close by, never. A hand folded message was given to the Prime Minister. The Planetary Council Advisor's offices in London and their quarters were empty. "Whether or not they return", she was saying, "deprnds on what you do in the next seventy two hours Prime Minister. Any attempt against advisors still on earth will result in severe repercussions." Danielle was telling him "If the Crown wanted to resolve this issue favorably then the Queen came aboard the Long Island. The Captain would show and allow her security forces to be in attendance. Seventy two hours Mr. Prime Minister, after that, depending on the Crown's response would determine if the council's advisors permanantly left Great Britain or not." The slur was not lost on the Prime Minister. Before he could respond the connection was broken off.

He was the first Prime Minister to deal openly and publicly with other worldly beings and their representatives. The tabloids were privy to the conversation unbeknown to him and the banner headlines the next morning were stinging. News channels and international television networks started countdown clocks. Still cloaked Alina had the ship assume orbit over the Lunar City to await the decision. This time she remained aboard during the entire seventy two hour period and refrained from going down to the surface. The scientific and retail communities were adamant that the Queen apologize. Their industries had seen phenomenal growth financially and in job growth since the advisors showed up. Scientific advancements were coming in waves. Advancements that would have taken hundreds of years to accomplish were happening in days instead. Parliament was seeing amazing drops in unemployment numbers and the country's gross national product numbers were never higher. Global requests were on the net for qualified people to fill thousands of jobs that England couldn't fill. Paleontologists from earth chewing at the bit to get to World Two Terra were told their plans were on hold depending on what happened in the next seventy two hours. In orbit over the planet they were powerless to go down. A few tried every possible con they could to go down but the command by the Captain no one transported down until a decision was made stopped them. So close and they could still be sent back to earth. All they could do was watch the planet from orbital space. Captain Davis was holding off on his order of continued restricted contact with England until the decision was made. The PM is the true power of the British government. An official apology by the Crown would fo;;ow in a few hours. The Queen would be advised of her apology to the Captain when it was made public.

A Decision Changes Everything

~𝔖~

T HE DECISION WAS flashed around the globe with viral speed. "Apology to the Captain" greeted the Crown when the morning paper was brought to the Queen. Within hours the council advisors returned to their offices and quarters and their normal class schedules resumed. It took near miraculous ability by the PM to convince the Queen that the decision was made for England's best interest. Sorry it offended the Crown but there was more to consider than the palace's feelings. The paleontologists aboard the Lincoln rushed aboard the battle craft as soon as the decision was made public. All had a supply of laptops with empty hard drives. The amount they would learn would no doubt fill every drive and then some more. Text books would be scrapped and all new text books written. Many careers of these people would be won here. Albeit with the nature of the research some would not survive to leave the planet. World One Sam was not even mentioned or named in any conversations. Animals and insects from the Devonian period on earth forward lived on the planet. Biochemists, botanists, biologists, toxicoligists, Paleontologists and every specialty of science was represented from many worlds. Survival was a minute by minute concern. Most knew this research project was a one way trip. The ships could take them back and forth, living to the end of their assigned tour was an uncertain propsition.

Alina was in her quarters when the decision was made known to her. She called Staerr to her quarters for a task and within minutes she was talking to Mike and Tony at the same time about this development. Davis had reinstated full contact with England when news of the apology was relayed to him. On Terra Two after only two weeks almost a third of the researchers found their way to being a dinosaur's dinner. All field research stopped until some way to survive here was found first. Advisors from the Tarnet Command stepped forward with a solution. Animals on their planet, very similar to the life here, were on their home world. Cloaking shields allowed them to move through areas where the larger animals were. The insects on their home world however, could sense them through the shields and attack even if they could not be seen. The cloaking shields were not a perfect solution but until something better was found, would let them work with relative safety. Fascination with the animals at first was replaced with a healthy dose of respect and fear of them. Occassionally a research team would find human remains in the field and return them to the research compound for identification and return to earth for burial. For all the danger and demonstrated risk of lives lost there was a waiting list of researchers to go to both planets pages and pages long.

The media was not left out of the picture to go to the planets, nor were they left out among the dead found or missing. Drones were snatched from the sky by Pterodactlys or some type of flying insect that was gigiantic in size. Robots that were designed to roam the area at night or during the day had a bad record of being stepped on and crushed by some of the larger ones. Teams of armed men and women with heavy weapons would accompany the researchers into the field. Hunting threats here was unlike any combat zone on earth. The animals were proving far more intelligent than originally thought, they could communicate, plan and coordinate attacks, were fearless and more often than not, hungry all the time. Humans they discovered was a nice addition to their food choices. Slow, almost deaf, slow to learn, defenseless and relatively stupid were easy kills. The researchers and armed team members that survived more than a month were considered old timers.

The experienced team members learned to use their sense of smell on patrol. Some animals had a particular odor and they learned what these animals were. The whole area was filled with hundreds of smells but only a few were of dangerous creatures. These were the ones they picked out and prepared to fight or hide from. Being on these two planets was an excercise in daily survival skills. Some of the larger insects, the team members that survived would learn, made unique sounds when they moved through the brush or flew overhead. Key sounds that they hear even in their sleep when they can get some sleep. On Atlantis it was a matter of being able to survive outside a submarine and though the sea life could not be heard or smelled, recognizing them by shape, preferably for survival sake at a distance from the diving party. Sea snakes are the size of Reticulate Pythons on earth. Megladon sharks on Atlantis are the norm not the exception. Harmless sea weeds on earth will swallow you whole on Atlantis. Shadows in the sea are usually, except for sharks, not a concern on earth. On Atlantis seeing the shadow first could save your skin. Gigantic cousins of the Manta Ray on Atlantis have found humans long term meals. The Merpeople have all gotten used to these dangers and take them for granted as an everyday risk of being on Atlantis. Humans have had considerably more diffuculty adjusting to the conditions on the planet.

On Atlantis the shores of the only continent on the planet are usually considered safe. There are of course those pesky sea weeds that will eat you coming right up to the rocks. Under the sand just off shore and into the deeper parts of the coast exist small fish whose stingers are venomous to humans. Prepare them wrong in cooking and the death is quick and there is no antidote. Not yet anyway. Terra and Atlantis are not a paradise by any stretch but they are lving examples of how life can develop when left alone for milliniums and milleniums times millenia. Terra, without the influence of man's interference, could be earth in it's natural development. The asteroid that killed the dinosaurs sixty five million years ago could have sparked the rising of a different form of life to rule the surface world. We will never know what could have been. Perhaps the primates on Atlantis's continent will the land for all time. If they can survive the other life forms on the continent.

The researchers on both planets must learn to live with the planet's inhabitants in order to live to the next day. Science only teaches you so much. Survival teaches you more of everyday living. The animals have learned where the humans are and how to get to them. The researchhers and security teams have to learn how to detect and avoid these predators in the compound if they want to live to learn more about them. Valuables are replaced with those things that you can hold close to you. Gold and silver mean nothing on either planet. Valuables become photographs and recordings from earth. If they die it is all their families and friends have left of them. These are their treasures. Gemstones, silver and gold are not edible and will not protect them from the planets indigenous life forms. The brain's ability to learn becomes the main weapon. When survival is uncertain the team members and resaearchers find relationships are not just superficial. Each could hold the other's life in their hands.

On earth life seems to go on as it did before the betrayal. Advances are made in every field of science at a phenomenal rate. Many beleive these advances are coming to fast for humanity to cope. Genetically specific cancer cures no longer raise an eyebrow. Designs in space science and equipment upgrades on the International Space Station make the station of even a few months ago seem antiquated and ridiculous technologically. With the advancements made on the I.S.S. solar panels were no longer necessary. Studies conducted by the council's advisor's assissting NASA concluded that a Ilaric propulsion system was ideal for the I.S.S.. Size and stress factors considered the Ilaric engines permitted the station to become a dedicated orbital weather satellite increasing the station's lifespan and effectiveness. Now able to fly on command to any region of the globe the station could track any weather system wth absolute precision. No longer all earthly equipment many cultures provided their technology for the station. Tarnet radar provides minute details of a storm's composition. Ilaric engines gives the mission commander the ability to move anywhere around the globe on his whim. Cenlian equipment provides detail chemical composition of the storm's molecular makeup and transmits that information in real time to any weather station or country that needs it. Construction on the I.S.S. was never ending. Crews operating from battle craft and repair drones were making adjustments and installing new compartments and data receptors on a continual basis.

UFO activity was kept at bay by the battlecraft and the council's ships, one or more were consistently in orbit about the planet and protected the crews working on the station. Space was a new frontier and with the advancements being made would certainly not be the last. Mankind, learning how violent a planet or planets can be, were only taking baby steps into a vast universe where any thing could happen. Questions answered only brought a hundred more questions. The first researchers and team members on Terra and Atlantis were nearing the end of their assigned tours. Most declined to leave. Some in a constant state of fear were ready to leave last week. As unusual as it sounds by the time the teams assignments were up they were just getting used to the planets. This was not the time to leave. The security team members senses were so acute and developed that going back to earth would be a mistake. Here they were alive and their very existence depended on the senses and knowledge they attained. Finding the remains of researchers and team members that were missing was still almost a daily occurance. Guards in the compound never relaxed because the next corner might hide a raptor or another animal eager for a slow moving meal.

We're Not In Kansas Anymore

PRIME MINISTER BROWN had been taking considerable backlash from the Royal Family. Calls of removal from office were being heard in both houses of Parliament. The Crown apologizing to a mere Captain even if the ship was a spaceship was intolerable. The Crown did not apologize to anyone. Monitoring the newscasts in England Alina decided to make things abundantly clear to the Palace. A gathering of the Royal Family was to be in three days, an event sure to be telecast around the globe. The PM would be there as a required but unwanted guest. A message on his desk was waiting for him that simply said "Remember what happened in Kansas."

Recent news on the television stations said nothing of any incidents in Kansas. Brown was at a loss to understand the message. It is the eve of the Royal Family gathering and leaders from around the world are invited to share this celebration with all of England. Reports of a tornado funnel forming in southern England is claiming the airwaves. Tornadoes? Kansas? Brown was beginning to see the picture unfold in his mind's eye. This was not a good idea. Before he could warn his security team they were aboard the Long Island. Danielle was waiting for them and she welcomed the Prime Minister aboard and said the Captain's were waiting for him. Captain's? This was not going to fare well. The Tretret were on edge for some reason. Another bad sign for what was going on, what ever it was. Entering a large room he saw before him in a row like judges eight of the Council's top Captains. Captain Grant was in the center of the group with Captain Davis on her left and Captain Williams of the Illinois Lincoln on her right. He would have to remember his name. The Tarnet Commander next to Tony then the Volitny Captain. On Davis's left was the Bolterer Captain and someone he did not know or recognize. To be with them he was obviously also a Council ship Captain. The Antarran ship's Captain was next to the Volitny Captain.

"Why am I here like this? Am I on trial?" he asked. A Strefden blade almost cut his throat it was lain so close to it. "You will speak to them with respect. Understand?" Put that way the meaning was clear. "Captains, why am I here?" "We have been monitiring your newscasts and feel it is time things were made clear to the Crown. You recieved the message?" "He responded that he had indeed recieved the message and asked if the weather anomaly in England was their doing? He could see a Strefdan start to raise his weapon and put his hand up to stop it. "The weather anomaly in the south is unusual for England. Why is it happening?" The Strefdan was becoming irritated at the PM's tone in his questions. Alina raised her hand and all stepped back. "Yes, we are controlling your weather in the south. Our way of getting your government's attention peacefully." Brown was going to say something but the Strefden and Tretret's attention were centered on him. "Captains, why am I here? I have not offended you to my knowledge", risking a Strefdan strike he continued, "yet you treat me like an Orion prisoner."

The Tarnet Commander started to rise his eyes becoming a dense gray. Alina told him to sit down she would handle this. "If you want him to treat you like an Orion he would be happy to do so. You are not on trial Mister Prime Minister, however," Brown waited for the other shoe to drop, "we have come up with a way to demonstrate to the Crown we are not to be betrayed and belittled. What happened in Kansas Mr. Prime Minister when a tornado touched down?" His gut suddenly dropped as he began to fully understand what was going to happen. "Your Crown and select members of your Parliament are going to see the other side of the rainbow Mister Prime Minister. And you," pointing to him, "will be right beside them to explain what is happening. Your security team and several of your Royal Marines will be with your party." He was going to ask a question and he was standing in a hallway off of the main ballroom where the celebration was in full swing.

Explaing this was not going to be easy and since there was no window of occurance on this plan when everyone just disappeared was an unknown. Political repercussions did not matter to the Captains or the Planetary Council. This was earth, let them deal with their own minor problems. He found a piece of paper in his pocket with several names on it. The Queen, by nature of her age and health, was not on it. The Princes were on the list.

Several Lords and six members of the House of Commons were on it. The best way to handle this was head on and the PM demanded an emergency meeting of both houses of Parliament and that it be televised. With no clue or indication of what this meeting was about the media was as stumped as everyone else what was to be discussed. If sensationalism sells papers this was going to be a sell out five times over.

The PM's demeanor was the first indication this was a serious matter and had to be addressed immediately. "During the Royal Family Jubilee," he began, "I was transported aboard the Long Island to face eight of the Council's senior Captain's. A few hours previous to the Jubilee I recieved a note that said 'Remember what happened in Kansas.' then the news reports of the tornado funnel forming in southern England was all over the news. I can see the light of understanding in many of your faces. I spoke with the Princes and described the situation in detail in a closed meeting the next morning. Hesitation was of course spoken of as any one might expect. The short of the message is that the Princes and several members of the Parliament, and I have a list of names here, will as the Captains put it, see the other side of the rainbow. There is not, I emphasize there is not a time set for this to happen. I will be contacted prior to this and those who refuse will not be taken. "These," "he raised the note with names up for all to see," are not required to go, in a sense it is voluntary. Those who agree will see wonders of this universe you cannot fathom in your deepest imagination." Turning to the media cameras set up for this he said, "There are also names of reporters and news anchors on this list. As before it is voluntary. Divided between the Long Island and the newest ship the Illinois Lincoln those on this …excursion, will see different parts of space and planets than the other ship."

He had to wait for the clamor to die down before he could continue. "The Princes are all for it much to the displeasure of their grandmother. I might place in here that MI-5 and MI-6 are against the members of the Royal Family going on this. You have heard of the new planets Terra and Atlantis in Queen Three about fifteen light years from earth. The ships can traverse that distance in approximately eleven earth hours by essentially bending space. For those going there are over three hundred fifty different lifeforms aboard the Long Island. There are over four hundred eighty sentinet life forms aboard the Lincoln. I will caution you now. Do anything, anything at all that threatens the Captains or try to talk to the Captains without invitation you will not survive. I cannot emphasize this enough. The dogs you see aboard are called Lomgren. They are extremely intelligent to the point they can have conversations with you," he paused for emphasis," and their bite is venomous. An animal the size of a rhinocerous will die withhin two minutes. There is no antidote to their venom. The giants you see everywhere are called Tretret and will without hesitation crush you. They do not know what fear is. They have never experienced it. Their primary function is to protect the Captain and their second in command."

A Lord stood and asked," You said the Lincoln had over four hundred eighty sentinent beings on board yet there are three hundred something members of the Planetary Council if I understand correctly." "You are correct. The other lifeforms on the Lincoln were saved by the ship from situations on their home planets and they asked to be crew members. The final decision is always the Captain's, no exceptions. The Captain agreed to their becoming part of the crew and they continue to serve with distinction. There are lifeforms aboard the Illinois Lincoln that horror movie producers cannot begin to believe exist, yet they talked with me like old friends when I was aboard." He regretted the mistake mentioning that as soon as it was said. You could hear the whir of a fan it was so quiet. "I will be advising those who choose to go when I am contacted." With those closing words he stepped down and hurried from the Parliamentary building. The repercussions, no matter how it was viewed, was going to be tantamount to political war between he and the Crown.

The name list was published in the newspapers and included reporters and anchors from every free world country. Camera crews of minimal size were allowed for each one. Sent by normal means their reports would not reach earth for thousands or millions of years in some cases so the reports were accumulated for broadcast when they returned to earth. Movie producers, script writers, toy manufacturers and model making companies were on pins and needles waiting for the ships to be seen in orbit over the earth. It was certain that the reporters and anchors would have a different image of their universe by the ships return. In some cases the news stations would take weeks assembling a special that made sense. Trying to quantify the information they accumulated was a task never attempted before. How do you take this information of the reporter or anchor talking with a lifeform from a different world and have five or ten more listening? Your anchor is landing on another world to step onto a planet that humans have never heard of much less seen and they are examining this new world with their own eyes. The reporter is on Terra and walking among dinosaurs and creatures dead millions of years on earth and the producer has to make a sensible report from this footage.

An anchor is standing in the viewing room of a submarine on Atlantis with ruins thousands of years old behind them and half human half aquatic creatures swimming at these incredible depths coming right up to the submarine curious about these odd creatures inside it. Producers and writers are trying to piece all this information together and still believe what their own eyes tell them. Interviews with the researchers on the respective planets are so filled with incredulous events that it is difficult to understand until a raptor or a winged insect four feet long tries to take them. Arthropods more than six feet long hunting them as they are reporting adds a new aspect to the job. Cameras finding human remains in the field hits home how dangerous this planet really is. The size of dinosaurs in real life wakes up the crews in a hurry.

On worlds so very far from earth those who chose to go are filled with sights and sounds that they will never forget. They are reminded these things they see are not even a layer of cells on skin to what is waiting in the universe. The Princes are fascinated by what they see, hear and learn. Sometimes with almost tragic consequence. These animals don't know royalty or care. Humans have been found to be easy prey taking very little effort on their part to track and kill. Their young don't care if it is an animal that is normally on their diet or an errant human or two that gets careless. In the months the survivors on either planet there has not been any human births. No one wants to bring a child into environments like these.

Danielle coordinated with Danella and Carin to have a Condition three alert while the guests are aboard to bring home that not all the dangers are on a palnet's surface. Anchors are recording a report for broadcast later on earth when battle stations were sounded. "All hands to battle stations. Secure visitors in safe areas, weapons to full power, medical bay stand by for casualties". What seemed to be chaos they began to see as practiced drills and soon the call of all battle stations were manned and reporting ready. Captain Grant came into the room where the reporters were and a call from

Danielle that three battlecraft were manned and ready for deployment her command. She acknowledged the report and asked if everyone was OK. Telling some of William's security team to make sure they stayed safe she hurried back to the bridge with the giant creatures they came to know close on her heels. They were still recording as they felt the ships aspect change and were forced to grab something to hold onto. They were uncertain what was happening when they heard torpdoes being fired and the ship shuttered from an apparent impact.

A call for medics to bridge immediately told them was not a drill they were at war with someone or something. The overhead speakers said that damage control was being sent to deck four section fifteen for hull breach. They heard the command for battlecraft deploy, set for hostile boarding of enemy vessel. Many reporters were speechless after all this was their first interplanetary attack. Medics entered the room where they were asking if anyone was hurt. A female reporter was having chest pains and was transported to the medical bay without a moments hesitation. It seemed as quickly as it had begun it was over. Except for the battlecraft the ship was returning to normal. Some of William's team were dragging creatures of some type away. A reporter asked where they were being taken to. He was answered to section four. Staerr came into the room where they were and said the woman was in surgery. The medics were repairing her heart. She should be back to normal in a few days well before their return to earth. An anchor asked her what section four was. "That is the prison section on the ship. I think you on earth call it the brig on a ship except section four has much more intense security measures."

Another asked what the creatures were being taken away. "They are surgically altered Orions. You don't want to know them. Did you smell them as they passed? That is normal for an Orion. Their normal appearance is much more unpleasant to the eye." Looking around the group of gathered reporters, camera crews and anchors she asked if they were getting adequate subjects for reporting? More than a hundred hours between each of them would have to be whittled down to just the essentials for broadcast. On the overhead the report of the battle craft were returning with casualties aboard each of them. Alina leaned back in her chair and told Danielle to set course for the Lunar City. She was losing too many of her crew and friends. The cemetery would get larger still. Once more they felt the ship change aspect and turning. Staerr said they were returning to the Lunar City. They had dead to lay to rest in the Captain's cemetery.

The caskets were lined up on the deck of hangar six. Each had the name of the treasured dead on it. Some sere small and others were gigantic in size. The reporters were asked to remain silent while the Captain was present. She knew each of those lying before her. Davis walked up to her and she pointed to two that Davis knew from when he commanded the Long Island. Tony stood by her and was quiet respecting their privacy in this time. Captain Davis went to the two Alina indicated and placed a hand gently on the caskets. He seemed lost in thoughts only he could have of these two. Looking at the others one or two he would stop at. He would not allow himself tears but the cameras clearly picked up tears from Alina. Other Captain's the reporters had come to know would be beside Alina and shake Captain Davis's hand, their words were lost to them but the message was clear. Centaurs carried the smaller caskets aboard the battle craft with the gentility of carrying a small child. They did not try to hide their grief. In life the Lomgren and the Centaurs badgered the other terribly but the dedication to the other was unquestioned.

Environmental suits had been provided the media before the ceremony would take place. Boarding a battlecraft designated for them they lifted off from the Long Island. The knowledge they would be on the surface of the moon was an overwhelming concept to think of. Certainly none of them had even considered the possibility. The battlecraft settled onto the lunar surface and they rechecked for the third time the media personnel's suits before the hatch was opened. Stepping onto the moon many were seized by a sense of panic and wonder at the same time. Walking to the cemetery the cameras captured the sign tha Alina had erected for those laid here. Remaining in the background mainly because a Tretret would block their attempt to move up to photograph, they recorded as much as they could. The cameras picked up other ships approaching the Lunar City landing near the cemetery entrance. Lifeforms they had never seen before greeted Alina, Davis and Tony like old friends. The ceremony aboard the Long Island was short but the respect the other Captain's and crew members showed the Captain was undeniable. On the surface the media was having trouble with the sudden change in gravity. As before Alina would go to specific graves and stay for many minutes at a few. As they prepared to leave a masive obstruction blotted everything else out on the cameras. The Tretret was pointing back to the ships waiting to take them back to the Long Island and Illinois Lincoln.

In this gravity the Tretret would have no trouble throwing them back to the ships if they dallied too long and take no small pleasure doing it. During the ceremony aboard the Long Island and again on the surface of the moon the Prince's were allowed to be close to Alina and the other Captains. Alina standing with the Prince's pointed to her right just as the earth was rising on the horizon. They and the media were stunned at watching the earth rise. Experiences none would ever forget and the knowledge that the producers would have to cut all this down to the 'essentials' was a task they did not want any part of. Earth was close enough to see and England was just coming into view. Pangs of regret were on everyone's hearts that they had to go back. It was going to be wonderful being home again but that emptiness would be present for a time too. When they looked into the sky they would see a much different view of the stars. The reporter with chest pains was among those on the surface of the moon and would never forget the wonderous beauty she could have missed. The question of what happened to the Orion was never brought up and the Tarnet preferred it that way.

Aftermath Of A Dream

BACK AT HER anchor's desk the reporter with the heart repair is looking over the notes by the writers. She tears the notes in half and casts them about the floor. Someone tries to pick them up and she sternly tells them to leave them. The producer's box asks what she just did and she bites back saying leave her alone. "Oh, and by the way thank you for noticing I had heart surgery in space and asking how I am doing." "Ok Cindy, how are you doing?" "Really Corey? I just told you I had surgery in space. My heart is better than it has been in years. Tell the cameras to follow me wherever I go, just follow me." In her ear piece she heard, "I liked the old Cindy better." "Carl, shut your mouth or I'll slap you through a wall." "Just out of curiosity how many here in the studio or of my colleagues have survived an attack by another planet's inhabitants? Let me see a show of hands. I see the hands of those on the Long Island and the Lincoln. Anyone else? No? Well we did. We met lifeforms we could not have thought up in a drug induced trip. We", she was trying to gather her thoughts, "experienced things in space and saw things that will never leave us. We learned that compassion is not just a human or earthly emotion, we saw compassion from beings that we call friends form other worlds. Respect is apparently a universal thing because we saw it time after time after time when the Captain's were facing personal losses. I spoke with some of the crew on the Long Island and learned there was an incident where the Captain was forced to fake her death." She was walking around the set and it was if she was feeling the emotions of the crew all over again. Tears were flowing from her eyes and she struggled to maintain her composure.

"I uh, heard how some of the crew cried openly when they thought the Captain was dead. Several were inconsolable to the point they died from grief. They are buried," she pointed to the moon, "up there in a cemetery that was built by the Captain." The studio was silent and no one was moving around their attention riveted on Cindy. "We saw in other lifeforms from other worlds that which we hope is the best in us. When it was discovered that the Captain was alive her Tretret commander, the giant creatures that follow and protect her and Danielle, were overcome with joy to the degree they cried tears. Although cry might be the wrong word to describe how they show emotion. I have tried to find a way to put it into words and I cannot begin to do it. They look into a person's eyes and it is how they confirm their identity. These giants are the most loyal and devoted creatures I have ever seen. No, that is not true. When it comes to the Captain the Strefden and the Lomgren are equally as devoted. The entire crew shows this devotion to the Captain." Cindy was still wandering about the studio only pausing for a few moments in one spot for the cameras to focus on her. "We saw an example of courage that to this moment takes my breath away. A Lomgren, a friend that looks like a Shepard, was with us on Terra. He reacted moments before a snake the size of an Anaconda on steroids struck. Rikea, his name, struck before the snake did. His venom caused the snake to convulse but Rikea," and here she could not maintain her composure and cried remembering her loss of a friend, "Rikea died protecting me. Rikea's venom killed the snake so I say to the snake, stick it up your ass." Sitting on the edge of the stage she stood slowly and turned to where her chair was.

The international news agencies had been broadcasting her every move and word. "My friend Rikea is buried up there with the honored dead. The sign at the entrance of the cemetery says that those buried here will never be forgotten again." Still with her eyes downcast in sadness she looked up at the camera in front of her. Tears still marked her cheeks. I recently purchased a German Shepard puppy and named him Rikea. It is my way of honoring and keeping Rikea alive in my heart. When we were aboard we were attacked by an enemy called the Orion. I can tell you that the odor they emit is worse than Carl's aftershave." Without missing a beat she said, "In the attack another Lomgren remained at my side and refused to move away from me. When the Orion was somewhere close by I could see his hackles rise and his teeth and fangs were bared. Venom dripped from his fangs when the Orion was brought through." Turning to the monitors in the studio she asked if any of the other correspondents had found out what happened to the Orions. No one had even stopped to ask. "Dangers," she continued, "are not only on a planet's surface as we found out and they will and do take those we found as friends. How do you describe the violent beauty of space in a way that those who have not ventured there can understand?" She shook her head in a manner that showed she felt there was no possible expression of what she knew from being there.

She looked up and there was a smile in her eyes, the first so far in this monlogue. "I saw on the Long Island Lomgren and Centaurs badgering the other like they were the deepest of enemies but turn around in battle and the other fights as fiercely for the other like they were the best of friends. I began to understand with a small sense of shame on my part that sometimes we do the same for others but don't know why. Shame because I was blinded by my own silly preconceptions about others that I failed to see them for who they are. I had to leave this world, almost die in a ship light years from earth, lose a very dear friend to a wretched piece of trash Orion to learn what life was about and see myself in a new light. As my colleagues in the control room can attest to earlier I have changed since my return. My heart attack on the Long Island was the best thing that could have happened to me. I was forced on that operating table as I was recovering to see the woman I was and see the woman I needed to be. Death, almost my own and the loss of some I call friends in that wonderous place called the Long Island, made me see that I am the least of all. I suffered the loss of friends in that attack and I still and will always grieve for those I lost. My sweet Rikea, I will miss him the most. What a marvelous person he was."

"Did you know that there are cats in space? There are indeed. The ones I met and spoke with, don't think me gone mad here because I am not, are part of the propulsion and star navigation engineers aboard the Long Island, New Iberia and the Lincoln." She started laughing and said "Rikea could not stand them. He told me the best cat was the one in his paws as he ate it." She laughed some more then almost too low for the microphones to pick up she said, "Oh Rikea, I miss you." Leaning against the front of the desk she looked directly into the camera without seeing it and said, "The universe we see from here is tiny, insignificant in the scope of reality. There was supposed to be a script I was to follow but I tore it up," indicating the papers on the floor, "as you can see. A script cannot say what needs to be said. Printed words don't come from here." touching her heart, "scripts are someone else's idea of what should be said. I could not do that this evening. I had to speak from what my heart told me to speak. Maybe some think me mad as a March hare for speaking as I have. Stick it where it hurts the most if you do. I don't care. Those of us who were on those ships, saw what we did, met and talked to the crew members we did and made the friends we did and," her voice softened, "lost the friends and colleagues we did are the ones who know what dangers are present out there."

"It was necessary to go the planet Cemok to pick up engineers to work on the propulsions system. Now these engineers are special. The Cencians are unique in that they actually live in the engine section. The radiation in the engines feeds them like we eat foods. It, according to the Captain, is a symbiant partnership between the Cencians and the council. Transported directly into the engine section they work on the engines and then are transported back to their homeworld when the work is completed. Highly radioactive themselves they have no enemies. Their world would kill an enemy in seconds if there was an invasion."

Turning to a physician on the stage with her she said, "Dr. Cambera I am going to put you on the spot. After seeing these things we did on the Long island would you define what life is? Hundreds of life forms on the ship wanted to talk to us to find out more about humans and this thing called imagination. Do you remember talking with the Centaurs that evening?" "Of course I do. They were incredibly intelligent and…. aware of things. I know that may be confusing to some but their awareness of us and the qualities humans possess and quite frankly we take for granted. It is not until you talk to people from another world that you realize how different we are from others. I spoke with a group of Sinefors, with the help of a translator, and they are fascinated by humans. Our world has life forms in the sea they cannot begin to understand how they live. Cuttlefish for example are a constant source of curiosity to them. The coral reefs we think are beautiful and take for granted they spend hours just looking at not sure what they are seeing. It is alive but they don't know why. The myriad of insects we have are a quandry of mystery for them. From the smallest ants to the largest of insects are very large questions to them. As to the definition of life, I was trying to apply the earthly definition to the creatures and civilizations we met and it doesn't fit. We have to redefine what life, and what makes something alive, really is."

Cindy stood and walked to the left side of the set and turned to the cameras, "I think Dr. Cambera will agree with me here. I kept making the mistake of equating another worlds people with the human measurement of intelligence. Big mistake on my part. Yes, it is the only measurement we have to quantify amother intelligence but when we do their I.Q. by earth standards is off the scale. Many of these civilizations are thousands and some millions of years older than humanity. On the Long Island those on the ship with us," indicating Dr. Cambera and her coleagues on the monitors ringing the set," we saw the most, I want to say awesome sight I could ever imagine. There is a ship in orbit around the Planetary Council's homeworld so massive it escapes any sense of reasoning. We were told it is fifteen hundred miles long and six hundred miles wide." Raising her index finger she continued, "Those measurements are not an exaggeration. To give you in the European community the enormity of this ship it is two thousand four hundred fourteen kilometers long by nine hundred sixty five point sixty one km wide. It has one hundred twenty one decks and is theoretically believed created to transport an entire civilization at one time. At those dimensions theoretically speaking, the populations of ten European nations would fit inside it and leave hundreds of miles of area empty."

"We were told the theory of why the crew and civilization it carried has not been found is because they possibly tried a core jump to travel to their destination quicker. The problem, it was explained to us, is dangerous because in a core jump everything and everyone aboard is killed. The researchers think they found some remains of those aboard in the cargo it carried and the hull and decks of the ship itself. The Captain of the Long Island held a memorial service for those that died on board and erected a placquard in their memory at the Lunar City cemetery. We don't know who or for that matter what they were but the Captain felt it appropriate that they not be just forgotten. That, I suppose, is the whole purpose of the Captain's cemetery. No one, or in this case, nothing is forgotten lost to the emptiness of time." Brushing a lock of hair from her eyes she was walking across the stage lost in thought about things known only to her. Shaking her head she said," I would not have traded my time on the ship for any reason. I understand that the Lincoln went to a different part of space and they saw worlds and wonders that rivalled any we saw on the Long Island. I find that hard to even conceptualize but space is a universe of incredible things."

"Cindy?" She turned to one of the monitors around her and said "Who spoke just now?" "It was me Angela. I was on the Lincoln and we were involved in two seperate attacks by the one you called the Orion. I agree with you they have a horrid odor about them, the Lomgren as with you, were ready to kill when they were captured. The Lincoln went by Terra and Atlantis and we saw things that escaped belief. The people on the Lincoln were so interested in talking to us that we barely had any time to ourselves and when we did we talked about the crew we had met and became friends with. You mentioned lifeforms on the Long Island that horror flick writers could not think existed in their wildest fantasies. I had the privalege of speaking to many of these creatures and what we take for granted is jaw dropping to them. I am a painter and was doing a sea side picture when a Crevalion came up behind me and asked where I saw these things. I told her I was just making up the pictures composition. She could not understand what I said. I think you remember Jerry from Galway, Ireland. We were on Terra and a worm of some type got a hold of him and killed him." Cindy's eyes began to fill with tears at hearing this. "I remember him well Angela. He had terrible jokes but he was a good friend. I feel so sad for his family. Another loss for me I will miss terribly." Cindy turned away from the cameras and used a tissue to dry her tears before she turned around again. Angela continued," We walked on a planet called Bretlia, completely uninhabited. There was no indigenous population on the planet." There was a rose I espied in the distance and asked the android with us what type of flower that was and she told me it was a Captain's Rose. Named after the Captain of the Long Island that first discovered it.

She would have to mark the rose's location on the planet. It was not believed to exist on any but one planet. Angela said that the android was no more forthcoming than that but she knew something was left out intentionally. Angela said, "You spoke of the knitting that bewildered the people on the Lincoln. Crafts as we know them on earth are so unique and many of the peoples we met can't comprehend imagination and creating something from the mind any time we want." "I know Angela I tried to explain creativity but they could not understand what I was saying. Like you I would sit down or just start drawing something and those with me would look everywhere to see what I was drawing. They were so puzzled that I could do that. Chris in New York, you are awfully quiet this time."

"Hi Cindy, I had the pleasure of being with you on the Lincoln though I stayed out of the way. Like you and Angela I met incredible people from other worlds. The conversations would go on for hours. The Sinefors were so interested in how we as humans could picture an event before it happened. They were absolutely stunned we can do that. I am sorry about Jerry and Rikea. My condolences for your loss Cindy. I think the Centaurs and the Strefden were my favorites on the ship." Angela cut in, "I can understand why the Strefden was one of your favorites. The Centaurs probably because most of the time you are a horse's…". Cindy interrupted here and said, "Be nice Angela."

Aboard The Long Island

ON THE LONG Island the Captain had the ship set course for Bretlia in David Four sector. The presence of the Captain's Rose in a supposedly inhospitable region of space was something she had to check out. As soon as the planet was within scanner range she had the ship slow and scan the planet with minute detail. Earth type atmosphere and a eighty nine percent equal gravity on the planet. Something was not right and Danielle, now knowing the Captain's mannerisms, asked what was wrong. "Send a scanning team with full surface team. Something just doesn't feel right. Be extra cautious on the surface and have them report directly to you every ten minutes." Danielle acknowledged the orders and a battlecraft was deployed to the surface. The surface team went first. The Cerollons taking to the skies immediately after landing. The rest of the team disembarked in order and the Lomgren were listening and smelling the air for anything they thought a threat. The Centaurs were right next to the Lomgren in full battle gear and armed. The Amdor's, the Strefden, the Medusan and finally the Tretrets stepped onto the planet surface. The scanning team disembarked last and following the Tretret orders stayed inside the protective circle of the surface team.

The Cerollons called down to the Tretret commander. They had company coming in on an interception course with the surface team. Another group was approaching from the left. A squeeze play to make the team surrender without a fight. Bad choice of tactic as they would discover. The scanning team was ordered aboard the ship and the hatch closed. The Cerollons themselves had not been spotted by the closing forces. One of the Lomgren got onto the back of a Centaur and sniffed the air for those closing in. Once he had their smell he could track them. They were noisy that was a downfall for them. As they closed they slowed and moved more quietly. Not quietly enough because the Lomgren had no trouble tracking them in the bushes. Just as they were going to try and attack the sound of wind whistling on wings caused them to look up and fire from the Cerollon's forced them to scatter. After that hey were easily picked off by the surface team. The skirmish was short and they threw their weapons down. The Medusan was in the front and looking imto their eyes was able to find out who they were and why they attacked.

They attacked believing they were an enemy that lived on the south ridge mountains. The enemy's description was the Orion down to the smell. A message was sent to the Tarnet Commander of an Orion battle camp on Bretlia. Within a days time the Tarnet ship was entering Bretlian orbit and after questioning the other force located the Orion battle camp. The Bretlians were told not to worry about their enemy anymore they would take care of them.

A negotiator from the Planetary Council was sent to Bretlia to determine the possibility of them being a member of the Council itself. They were decades from attaining the most rudimentary space flight capability. Still the Tarnet Commander pushed for membership for Bretlia. They had captured many of the most wanted by the Tarnet in the battle camp. The Bretlians would be taught more effective means of agriculture and water management, their medical sciences would take a massive jump in quality, their industrial capability would be much higher and the council would protect them. Other than that they would be helped when they needed it and left alone otherwise.

In the early morning skies above the skirmish site the Bretlians saw an enormous craft drop below the clouds amd creatures like they had seen before exit the ship. Then it rose silently into the air and hovered at about five hundred feet. A hatch in the craft opened and a solitary figure floated to the ground. As she descended the wind blew her hair about her shoulders and the morning sun was directly on her face. Alighting softly she went to the android that had identified the Captain's Rose. Looking at the flower in the morning sun the flower was clearly a different color yet the same variety as her rose.

It was difficult to measure the hatred for the Captain as opposed to the Tarnet by the Orions they were so very close in intensity. On the Tarnet ship Captain Davis reminded the Orions he was the one that set war on them and destroyed their home world not Captain Grant. It was forces under his command that destroyed their technology and it was he that ordered the destruction of the Orion ruling council. They clearly had issues to settle with Captain Davis and not Captain Grant. When they were ready to do something about that Davis would be waiting. The attacks against the Long Island and the Illinois Lincoln with the guests aboard were meant for the New Iberia. The Orion chose the wrong targets. If they had found the New Iberia first and attacked the Tarnet Command ship was twelve minutes behind the Iberia.

Tony was walking the hallways on deck eleven to explore his ship and meet more of his crew personally. It never ceased to fascinate him the different crew members he had and it was a pleasure he looked forward to on a daily basis to go to a different area and meet those there. Carin called him on his communicator he was needed on the bridge immediately. He walked onto the bridge and the call 'Captain on the bridge' had become a normal thing to him. On the screen was several what appeared as mountains floating in space with cities built on them. He ordered scans and there were massive life signs detected. Someone or something was very much alive on those floating cities. He had messages sent to any other council ships in the area for response. The Volitny Commander and the Canteranian ships were in the region and reported they were enroute to the Limcoln's coordinates. Alina and Davis were quite a distance away and were monitoring the developments on the Lincoln. Both Captain's felt the aspect of their ships change and a new course set and engaged.

Still aboard the Long Island the negotiators for the council were advised of the Lincoln's discovery and they were enroute to see this amazing sight themselves. The negotiators asked if there was a single day they, the human Captains, did something that didn't cause the council a problem? Danielle answered them by saying look at the challenges they would miss out on without them. The Volitny and the Canteranian Captain's were nearing the Lincoln and could not believe what they were seeing. The life form readings were enormous in number. Communication attempts had so far not been returned. With that type of technology surely they knew the ships were there. Tony told Carin to try sending a message using other forms of communication, old style radio on carrier waves, flashes of light like morse code or transmit holographic images showing peaceful intentions. It seemed the morse code was understood and messages were returned to them. The

Dofgrara were transmitting at the same speed the mountain cities were transmitting. It took a short time to compile the differences between their code and the earth morse code but they were so similar it did not take long. Tony thought the similarity odd and quite likely not accidental. The code was transmitted to the other two ships so they could understand what was being sent back and forth. After a few hours of studying the code the other council ship's communications officer's had the language down.

When Alina and Davis learned of the morse code languages they were silent. Of all the wonders out here they had seen so far they thought nothing would surprise them but this, this had them breathless. Danielle and Danella were not sure how to read their Captain's. This was a reaction they had not seen before. A closed comunication between Captain's was requested by Davis to include all council ship Captain's in the region of the mountain cities. Returning to the bridge Davis told Danella to copy the morse code language sent by the Lincoln and for her to learn it as quickly as possible. The same instructions were relayed aboard the other ships. Alina was still silent except to find out time to interception point with the Lincoln. Alina directed the negotiators be brought to the bridge. When they arrived without saying a word she pointed to the communications console. One hesitated and started to say no when a Tretret arm picked him up and dumped him on the floor in front of the console. In a deep growling voice the Tretret told him, "When the Captain tells you to do something you do it. Refusal will result in an attitude correction session. Understand?" Alina looked at the negotiator and thanked her commander for the clarification.

Danielle told the other to say what he wanted the Dofgrara to send to the mountain cities. Be respectful and think before he sent a message. Angry at his treatment he tried to scold the Captain and two things happened almost at the same time. A Lomgren's jaws were almost touching his leg and a Strefden blade was laid against his neck. Alina said nothing and then reminded him that she was the Captain of this vessel and he had no authority aboard. He was a guest. A status she could recind at any time. Staerr looked at him and said coldly for him to do his job. A Centaur had moved next to the Lomgren where he always seemed to be. The glare in his eyes was clear enough warning that the negotiator needed to change his attitude or die on the bridge. He would file a complaint with the council and the Captain told him that was his privilege.

The second negotiator pulled his colleague away from the station and told the Dofgrara to send folowing message. "This is Ankila, a negotiator for the Planetary Council aboard the Long Island. We are explorers and found you and your cities floating in space. Do you require any assistance?" The reluctant negotiator was unceremoniously removed from the bridge and escorted to a holding area well away from the bridge. The medics had to correct crushing injuries to his arms from William in removing him. "The message was returned they had an illness they did not have any way to stop. The negotiator said if they would permit the Long Island they could transport several individuals to their medical bay for examination. Perhaps the Long Island would have or could develop the medicine needed to help their sick." Alina called the medical bay stand by for ill patients, unknown type or life form. Isolation procedures. The chief physician called and said would be ready in six minutes to recieve patients.

A contingent of individuals accompanied the patients being sent to the ship and after being cleared by the medics were allowed to walk the halls. The negotiator was waiting for them and greeted them in the medical bay. They were humanoid. The patients were in isolation chambers and quickly diagnosed with a common type of flu. A few hours in the medical bay and they joined their colleagues in the hallways. A supply of medicine was gathered and then sent to the floating cities. Medics were sent to several of the floating cities to treat the more serious of issues. Those requiring surgery were transported to council ships and recieved the help required. Cities floating in space but didn't have all but the most rudimentary medical and technological development. The course the cities were headed on would take them into dark space in a few years at the speed they were going.

Engineers aboard the New Iberia were able to construct a makeshift propulsion unit for the cities that would take them into a direct course with the Planetary Council homeworld. In orbit the cities would not be wandering aimlessly and researchers in the council could study these remarkable mountain cities. The populations could be relocated to a different part of the Bretlian world so they would not interfere with the indigenous population. The life support in the cities would not last forever. Relocation was definetly the best option. Bretlia was already protected by the council and stations up and operating could provide power and water sources to both populations. Some questions that the human Captain's wanted answered was how did humanoids get into space in living mountain cities? Where did they originate? How old were their civilizations? The council researchers coud not say that the human Captain's didn't keep them occupied. Generations of mountain people had seen the other mountain cities float near them. They had no idea what they looked like or anything about these fellow wanderers. Bretlia would be the first time they would meet.

Creatures sent from the orbitting council ships gave the mountain people pause when they first saw them. When they discovered they could communicate with them it eased their anxiety a little. Still these were creatures from other worlds among them. A woman that was one of the mountain people was not watching where she was walking on this new world of Bretlia and walked into a wall of fur. Looking up there was an Amdor looking down at her. Startled she fell back and would have hit rocks behind her but his giant hand stopped her fall. He said, "Easy little human. You will hurt yourself." "What did you call me?" "You are a human little miss. We have ship Captains that are human. Many of us serve with them and that is how I know what you are." "Human? I don't understand what you are saying. I don't know what a human is." Maybe I need to have you talk to another human and maybe you will understand then." This was something Alina could not ignore. A completely unique opportunity to teach a new culture about their human heritage. The morning sun was rising and many of the new Bretlians were looking around still exploring their new home. Clouds, something they had never seen before was filling the sky and turning dark gray. Lightning flashes and thunder scared them and fascinated them too. As they looked skyward a large ship descended to just below the clouds and remained still and silent. More of the creatures that were becoming common to them now materialzed in front of them. As they watched a hatch opened and a solitary figure descended from the ship alighting softly on the ground. A woman with hair that was brown with shimmering reddish tones and shoulder length stood in front of them. They could not help staring, first at her beauty and second that she was like them. Alina greeted them and then said that like them she too was human. Tests conducted by her doctors on the ship showed human DNA traits. At the mention of DNA she recieved blank looks. They did not know what DNA was. This was going to take a very long time of contact that was obvious. "Just believe me when I say we share the same ancestry as you. You are human too."

A little girl stepped forward and said, "That is why you knew what to do when we were sick. You went through it too." The light of understanding began to show behind those pretty hazel green eyes. Alina could clearly see that his little girl was exceptional in intelligence and reasoning. "And when my momma was hurting from her chest you knew what to do.My sister has been sick all her life but you helped her be like me." Alina saw saddness enter her eyes and asked why she was sad. She said, "I don't understand." Alina had not laughed in a long time but this little girl was reaching her on a level that she herself had not explored yet. "It is called medicine little one. It takes years of education to learn and is very hard to do." The little girl came close to her and said there was things in the trees that scared her. Turning to the Cerollons she motioned up and to the trees. Rising into the sky the Cerollon flew to the trees and flew around them looking deep into their branches. A blast of fire from one of the Cerollons and Alina and the little girl were surrounded by a living wall. Motioning a Lomgren and Centaur forward they went to the trees and found the scary things in the branches. One of them dropped on the Centaur's back and was killed by the Lomgren's bite in moments. She motioned a Strefdan and a Tretret forward to back them up. When the Tretret was close to the tree another jumped on it and tried to kill it.His hand tore the creature from his back, threw it to the ground and then stepped on it.

The creature continued to fight and tried to topple the Tretret only to fail. The Treret picked up the creature and a massive fist sent it into the trunk of a neighboring tree. Howls from the other trees was immediate. Another tried to charge the Strefdan and met his blade mid air leap. The Centaur was fighting with two, the Lomgren killed the one he was fighting and then turned his fury on those attacking the Centaur. By this time some of Wiliiam's team was involved in the fight.. Without hesitation Danielle had Alina transported aboard the ship. Since she was holding the little girl both materialized on the bridge. The little girl's eyes were wide with wonder at what she was seeing. Her jaw dropped as she looked around. Staerr came to her and gently pushing her jaw up said, "Hi. What is your name?" Looking at her all she could do was point around her. "Yes this is the bridge of the ship." Indicating the Captain she said, "She is the Captain, in command of the ship. This is Danielle. She helps the Captain run the ship. What is your name?" "They call me Wendy, but my name is Winnifred." "Wendy, you have a pretty name. My name is Staerr. Are you hungry?" Wendy shook her head yes quickly and Staerr said, "Let's see if we can find something you like OK?" Taking her by the hand she took her off the bridge. Alina wanted to know what was happening. What are those creatures? Danielle answered that they are a type of Simian lifeform. "Danielle have several transported to section four. I want to see them myself."

As they were going through the halls toward section four Alina was deep in thought. Danielle, knowing her Captai's moods and expressions asked her what she was thinking. "Danielle what if those creature were transplanted on another planet like Terra Two? They are obviously very wild and a planet like Terra Two has plenty of food and water for them. I think they could quickly adapt to the planet. And the people on Bretlia would not have to be afraid to live there. Send an inquiry to the council as to the feasibility of my idea." When she entered section four the creatures, a dark graaish black with very coarse hair and teeth designed to eat meat were in a rage. About two meters in height William estimated their weight close to five hundred pounds for the smaller ones. Closer to eight hundred plus for the larger ones. Their fury seemed to be directed at the Tretret and ignoring the Captain. Tony had transported aboard and walked into section four. "You still get into trouble Princess. I think you look for trouble then call me to get you out of it." "Tony, how are you? What do you think of my find here?"

"Ok, so now what are you going to do with them?" "If approved I am going to transport the whole lot on Bretlia to Terra Two." "What the hell did Terra do to piss you off that badly?" She gave him the hurt look he knew so well. "Stop that Princess, it won't work with me." "I found something else on Bretlia too." "Now what? Is it dangerous too?" Staerr met them at the entrance to section four with Wendy holding her hand tightly. Alina pointed to Wendy. "This is Winnifred." "Wendy!" she was quickly corrected. Tony looked at Alina with that knowning what is coming look she knew well. Alina told him, "It wasn't until about an hour ago she learned that she and the people in the mountain cities are human. Did not even know what humans were until today." Ice cream stains on her dress was telling. "You start her off right. Ice Cream?" Wendy pointed to Staerr and said, "She said that it was chocolate. It was really good." "I'm sure it was. Where are your parents Wendy?" "They were in a empty place and went away." "The bubble keeping them alive was deteriorating and her parents were in an area that dissapated without any warning. Her mother's family is caring for her."

Alina recieved a message on her communicator about incoming messages from the council. With Wendy being kept busy with Staerr Alina could focus on her duties. "Captain," Danielle was speaking, "the researchers determined that the cities bubbles would dissapate long before reaching dark space. It would not have mattered to them. As to your inquiry it is approved so long as the creatures are located far from the research stations." Alina looked at Danielle and didn't see her she was lost in thought. "Danielle have the chief engineer brought to me would you?" After about fifteen minutes the ships chief engineer came onto the bridge. Alina talked with him in a low tone so others could not hear. She told him of the cities bubbles deteriorating. She asked him, "What if there is a mechanism inside the mountains that generates the bubbles. If you and your engineering team could look at them and see if they can be repaired. Someone made them because the mountain city people have very basic industrial skills. There is another civilization's work there. I want you and as many team members and specialty personnel as you need to look at them and see if they can be restarted." Turning away to see the screen she remembered the other matter. Turning back she said, "I have another task for you too. You have heard of the incident on the planet below?" "Yes, Captain I have. Three of my engineers were attacked and injured. Medics are working on them now."

"I am sorry for that. I will make it a point to see them. The creatures that attacked them, there are several in section four, I recieved OK to relocate all of them to Terra Two. Somewhere away from the research stations. You have clearance to use as many of the crew as you need to figure out how to do it. You have several weeks to figure it out. The population in Bretlia is under extreme threat because of them."

A few hours later Alina was told the Chief Engineer wanted to talk to her. When he came onto the bridge he said that the relocation was not going to be a problem. He had just come from section four and with the chief physician had calculated a dose of medicine to knock them out during transport. The operation would take several attempts since they couldn't get all of them in a single place at one time. The main thing that would take time was constructing special vehicles to hold them that could be towed by a ship to Terra Two. Never allowing them actually aboard a ship prevented some possibly tragic results. As bait to bring them aboard the vehicles Tretret or Amdor blood would draw them in numbers. She gave him the go ahead and to use the landing bays on decks eight, nineteen and forty two to assemble the towed craft. Telling Danielle she had the bridge she was going to medical bay to see those injured on the planet below.

The creatures in section four were transported back to the planet in a remote area to keep an escape from causing a tragedy. They were alive now but if one of her crew died as a result of their attack the consequence would be final. She went from one to the other stopping at some for several minutes to talk to those immediately around her. The crew knew the Captain cared about them and that made her different from any previous commander other than Captain Davis. She seemed to have no bottom to her capacity to caring. The three engineers were told of the plans to build specialized vehicles to transport the creatures to Terra Two. They would volunteer time to build and some of their blood to bait them into the vehicles. She stopped next to a Lomgren laying on a gurney, and no surprise to her, a Centaur was right next to him. She thought of the symbiant relationship of one lifeform with another. Symbiants they were not, but it didn't look that way.

She pulled a stool up to sit on and spent several minutes talking with both them. Speaking with a 'dog' and a Centaur was as natural to her as speaking to anyone else. Bandages on the Centaurs back looked like there might be a nasty wound under it. The medics came over at that time and they started working on his back. The wound from the simian's claws were deep and no doubt very painful but the Centaur showed no indication. She stopped the Lomgran from trying to twist around to see. She told him just to lay there and relax. His friend would be with him again in a little while. The Lomrgan's injuries were severe and while he would not die from them it would be close to a week before he left the medical bay. Every day other Lomgren and Centaurs would come see him. A Tretret or three and Amdor's made it a point to see him at least twice a day. He could not understand the Sinefor's but they too would visit. If someone did not know better they might think the crew was a family. More of the Long Island's engineers were being used for the project on the mountain cities. Orbiting the Planetary Council homeworld the Captain had to set position farther away from the planet than usual. The mysteries of the Constellation were being slowly solved and computerized glitches were corrected with the help of the Sinefor on the ship.

Speaking of which Alina noticed she didn't hear or see any on the bridge. "Danielle, where are the Sinefors? Normally there are several on the bridge." "Most are on the Constellation or on the mountain city projects. There are a few we can draw on still aboard if needed Captain." With all of the engineers and Sinefor's involved in the other projects her ship was not complete. Looking at Danielle she said, "Any possibility that engineers and Sinefors from other ships can be used? The ship doesn't feel right with them gone." Only a human Captain would miss the crew mwmbers working on the other projects. The Captain wanted her crew back. Instructions were sent for the chief engineer to return to the ship and report to the Captain. As he walked into the bridge the look in the Captain's eyes told him all he needed to know. "Welcome home." "Thank you, Captain. "Any possibility engineers and Sinefor's or other engineering personnel from other ships can be used here? Want to break orbit and I want all of my crew aboard. Doesn't feel right with so many gone."

"Danielle, tell the council I need all of my crew back aboard. Make up an excuse, lie if you have to." "Captain may I remind you I am an android I cannot do either of those things." "If I gave you orders to tell the council something would you follow my orders?" "Of course Captain, you know that." "Then tell the council we have recieved a distress call from the Titanic and are going to assist. Relay to the New Iberia and the Lincoln on your direct channel. They will understand." The Titanic? As far as Danielle knew there was not a ship in the council fleet with that name. When Danella and Carin relayed the message to their Captain's both reacted with laughter. Danella and Carin not sure what laughter was were beside them immediately asking if they were OK. Did the Captain need the medics? They waved them away they were OK. Tony told Loreen to send a closed message to the Long Island. At the same time one was being sent by Tanya to the Long Island.

"Captain, incoming messages from the Illinois Lincoln and the New Iberia deignated priority closed." "Send to my quarters Staerr." Turning her chair to Danielle's place on the bridge said she had the comm." "The Comm Captain? I have an incoming message?" "It means you have command. I will be in my quarters for a short time." Humans could be so confusing. Danielle thought she knew the Captain quite well and yet everyday some new facet of her was revealed. "The Titanic Princess? Really? That is an original excuse. I doubt very much the council has any information on the Titanic. I am sure they are really confused what the Titanic was." "I have to agree with Tony Alina. Completely original idea. I almost fell out of my chair I was laughing so hard." After a short time Alina walked back onto the bridge. Danielle said, "Message from the council Captain. What and where is this Titanic? We can send additional ships to assist if necessary." "Tell them not necessary the ship has sunk and cannot be retrieved." "Captain may I ask what does sunk mean?" "On earth ships sail on the open seas and oceans. When they are sunk they go to the bottom and all hands still aboard die with the ship." Message sent to council Captain. They don't understand message."

Danielle reported all of the crew were back aboard and ready for departure. "Have any other ships come through the dark space since we were there last Danielle?" I am told one has come through. Markings indicate it is an earth device. It is the head of a missle of some kind. "Get all ships away from it. It is a nuclear device with multiple warheads. Set intercept course with the missle and standby on weapons." How the missle got all the way out here was a mystery but one that would have to remain unsolved. Primary job now was destroying it before it killed others or a civilization got a hold of it and reverse engineered it into more just like it." Jump capability is authorized Danielle. Get us there as quickly as possible." During the flight to the dark space region the Captain was nervous. Kept asking how muuch longer until the ship arrived? Were weapons on standby at her command? "One minute to arrival Captain", Staerr said. "Drop from jump speeds. Standby to fire on my command. Belay that order." Belay that order? "Captain I do not understand that last command." Danielle was saying. "It means cancel it. Get the weapons section commander up here now."

When he arrived the Captain explained what they were facing and that the warhead was very old. It had multiple nuclear warheads and would not react well to being probed. The best option was to send the warheads into a star. Alina had Danielle set course for the nearest sun and towed the warhead behind the ship. She would not endanger her crew and ship for an antiquated device. Jump capability was at standby if things started to go wrong with the warheads. The closest sun's gravitational field was already affecting the ship. Once the Captain was assured the gravitational field would draw the warhead to it she had the tracor beam released and watched as it disappeared into the sun's corona exploding in a bright flash. Shields were up because of the blasts concussive force. "Initiate jump now," the Captain ordered. Before the concussive force could reach the ship it was far away.

She had the incident entered in the ships log and thought no more of it. Another day on the Long Island. Alina could hear overlapping communications coming in but the Dofgrara were not having any difficulty sorting them out and following each one. Anything of importance would be relayed to the Captain but this was just everyday routine communications. Danielle said, "Captain a request for addition to the Long Island crew is coming in from the Lincoln. A Koriat wants to join the crew. I know nothing of the Koriat at all Captain." "See what you can learn about them and get me a connection with the Lincoln Captain to Captain." Davis was included in the conversation because some wanted to serve on the New Iberia too. "Princess what a surprise. What can I do for you?" "Tony what are the Koriats like? Know nothing about them" "Well they look like Mike.." Alina cut in, "That ugly huh." "I heard that you two." he cut in. Alina feigned innocence, "Oh Mike, had no idea you were on." Danielle was perplexed. Of course she knew he was on. The communication required her orders to initate. Danella and Carin were not sure what was going on but the Captain's seemed to be OK with it. All three seemed to be having fun with this. "Seriously Alina and Mike. Koriats are hard working and have been a real boost to my crew. If you approve their inclusion in your crews you won't regret it. The men stand a little more than two meters tall and weigh about one hundred eighty pounds, muscular and look European. The women are about five and a half feet tall and weigh around one hundred fifteen pounds as average. Both are handsome in appearance and the men are skilled warriors in unarmed and hand to hand combat. In fact I put two Koriat's on my surface team and battle craft boarding teams. Close quarters engagements is where they shine as fighters. I have several people in my crew that want to transfer to your ships you have never even seen before."

Alina said, "Tony I will consider the Koriat's but need you to transfer information on the others to Danielle for her to examine and then we will discuss the transfers." "Same here Tony as far as the Koriat's. Danella will evaluate the others and then get with me on them." Danielle did not miss the trust the Captain had in her. Those that built them and then abandoned them for those endless years could care less. The Captain placed a lot of trust in her and she would not disappoint. Six Koriat couples transported aboard the Long Island and a preliminary board of Danielle, William, the Tretret commander and one of the engineers interviewed them first. Then they were interviewed by the Captain, Danielle and Staerr before approval for crew membership. All were approved with the understanding if they failed to measure up to crew standards they would be sent back to the Lincoln. As did Tony, several men were assigned the surface landing team and the other three were assigned to a boarding crew. In a offhanded discussion with others on the ship the Koriat's too had encountered the Orions and Sorians. They didn't think much of either of them and proved more than able to overpower them easily.

The Koriat women drew their enemy in with their charms and apparent vulnerability and then killed them. Excellent in the medical arts they were equally adept at killing quietly. The Koriat couples made friends with the other crew members and was soon accepted and included in other crew activities. The Captain and Danielle were wary of their ability to become killers in a moments time. In a combat simulation the Koriat's went against Tretrets and Strefden on a mat with a ring near the edge. The objective being throw or push your opponent outside the ring. Anxious to see these skills they supposedly possessed the Strefdan went first. He was easily thrown outside the ring by the Koriat. The Tretret now stepped into the mat and tried unsuccessfully to grab him. Tripping the Tretret he forced him with different attacks to step outside the ring. The Lomgren went next. He had been watching this Koriat and thought he knew it's weakness. A leaping attack only served for it to be grabbed by the Koriat and tossed effortlessly outside the ring. A Centaur bumped the Koriat knocking it down and apologizing for not watching where it was going extended a hand to help it up and continued by sending the Koriat flying outside the ring onto the deck.

"As you were!" The Captain had been watching and saw the Lomgran ready to kill. To the Koriat she said, "You are new to the crew so you don't know. Fight a Lomgran and you fight a Centaur too and vice versa." The Tretret Commander with her was also watching and marked the Koriat's actions and would find a way to counter them. This thing as he considered it could be an asset but at this point had his doubts and relayed his opinion to the Captain. She, not convinced the Koriats would fit in to the crew, agreed with him. Ordering the commander to watch them closely she would evaluate them on a day to day basis. Repeated assurances from Tony did little to quell her concerns. Those opinions and their loyalty to the crew would be tested in a real combat situation in a very short time. Danielle had been tracking an unknown contact on the scanners that remained at a distance of three hundred thousand kilometers and paralled the Long Island. Much smaller than the Long Island, about the size of a battle craft, it did not change course or get closer. Alina ordered a battle craft to intercept and board the unknown vessel. Danielle said repeated attempts at communication was futile, if they understood, they were not answering.

This would be the Koriat's first true test in a combat situation. As the battle craft approache the unknown vessel turned directly in their path intending to ram it. Avoiding the collision by an arm's length the battle craft used claws to capture the ship and draw it close enough to breach it's hull. Transporting aboard the vessel the Long Island's crew ran into an ambush. The Koriats fought with the intensity that the crew was sure was based on them knowing their enemy. They were correct. The enemy known quite well to the Koriat fought them with an intense hatred. Almost ignoring the rest of the boarding party was their mistake. The enemy wanted the Koriat dead no matter what or how many died. Lomgren killed several with bites and were still muchly ignored. Trertes and Strefden had never been in a situation where they were standing around in a fight doing nothing. The entire battle was centered on the Koriats dying. Two Koriats started to go down and a Strefdan using his blade killed the attackers. It seemed after that the enemy knew they were there and the fighting became a war in a small space.

Tretret fists would send one into a bulkhead and they would come right back and attack. This enemy was well versed in the combat arts and was a challenge from the first. Amdor's were being dragged down to the floor as the enemy tried to kill them with a knife of some type. Lomgren bites stopped the attackers but opened themselves to attacks. Centaurs enraged at the attacks fought with a blood filled intensity. Kicks by their legs sent some of the enemy into consoles and bulkheads and their weapons finished them. The Koriats had been fighting relentlessly since the boarding and the others started making headway into diminishing the enemy's numbers steadily. At some point there were more of the Long Island crew than the enemy but their attacks on the Koriat did not end until all were dead. The entire crew of the unknown vessel were dead. The Koriat's all had deep wounds and were bleeding from repeated stabbings. They were transported directly to the medical bay and moved into surgery as they arrived. There would be alot of questions about this unknown enemy and why did they hate the Koriat so terribly.

The bodies prepared for moving to the Planetary Council homeworld would have post mortem examinations, tried to be identified as to planetary origin and their technology, for now, remained on the Long Island. The ship's engineers, Sinefors and some of the feline engineers would be brought into tear the ship down to it's last connector and circuit. Analyze them and see if the technology was adaptable to the council's ships. The Tarnet Commander who had been monitoring the incident offered the assistance of some of his engineers to tear it down and examine every aspect of it's engines and weapons systems, which Alina noted, was never used against the Long Island. It was if they knew the Koriat were aboard and killing them was the purpose of this whole incident. Alina welcomed the Tarnet assistance and within minutes the landing bay on deck six was filled with people tearing the ship down and parts were scattered helter skelter on the bay floor. The Tarnet engineers were able to ascertain something quite quickly from the examination of the engines. This was a one way trip. They had no intention to return to their home world. As to the weapons the ship didn't have any. Alina and the Tarnet Comander knew right then this was to them a suicide mission. They were to kill the Koriat and destroy themselves afterward or all die trying, which they did. Planetary Council computers did have information on the Koriats, although sketchy, and a battle that left most of another world's inhabitants in ruin was in the records.

The courage of the Koriat's was no longer in question. Neither was the fact that during the battle they never asked for help from the other crew members in the boarding party. Danielle sent a message to Carin over their closed channel advising her of the incident. Tony asked the Koriat still aboard the Lincoln about this enemy. Yes they were quite faniliar with the Senlaria. Pillagers and murderers of their home world a war between the Koriat and the Senlaria erupted and their home planet left most of their population without homes, food, loss of industry and lives of their loved ones. That was one hundred forty two years ago and the war goes on. Carin's message to the council about the Senlaria did help shed light on a few things they were finding. Research into the history of the Koriat and Senlaria was revealing a history of cruelty and murder on both sides. The Koriat had a hand in this as much as the Senlaria. The Senlarian ships navigation computer showed the point of the ships origin. The Lincoln was closer and set course for Senlaria. Their scans sowed desolation and ruin covering the entire planet. Life sign readings were strongest in only three cities. Communications was not possible with the surface so Tony ordered a contingent of personnel with a council represenative to make contact on the surface.

When the scout ship landed a small distance from the largest of the three cities it was immediately apparent to the council represenative that the Senlaria did not have the ability to wage war of any kind with anyone. Amid the ruin and debris of the city the remains of the dead were still present. Here and there were small camp fires burning to keep the people around them warm and cook what little food was available even after more than a century. In contrast a council represenative found Koriat a bustling and prosperous world with plenty of food and industry. Shopping malls were filled to capacity with people buying and selling. No attempt to help the Senlaria was even attempted. The Planetary Council had another crisis on their hands brought about by the human Captains. That was not entirely true but the actions of the crew were directly placed on the ship Captain's shoulders. In this case on Tony's shoulders since the team was sent to the Long Island from his ship. Tony argued he was not responsible for what a life form on his ship did almost one hundred fifty years ago. The council judge's were forced to agree and acquitted Tony of responsibility. The Koriat were not yet members of the council so the council had no authority over them. The council would shoulder the Senlarian problem on it's own shoulders.

Of the the three hundred fifty member planets and systems of the council most responded with promises of assistance to the Senlaria home world. The Koriat home world refused to assist. Even earth was willing to respond and help. The United States would send aid workers to Senlaria if they were needed. It was agreed and a Bolterer ship picked up fifty eight volunteers to go the Senlaria. Warned that it was more like the devastation of Europe at the end of WWll, all reaffirmed their willingness to continue to Senlaria. Pallets and pallets of supplies, food and medicines were taken aboard. Since the Senlarian were considered humanoid in nature medical staff was hoping there was not too much difference in them from humans. To those going to Senlaria the mere fact they were humanoids was something they could not have known in their wildest fantasies. Another planet inhabited by relatives of humans? It was just so much to process at the time. If they had known of Bretlia they would have had more difficulty with at least two planets with human relatives maybe more out there?

The Long Island with the help of other council ships had transported as many of the simians to Terra Two in an area hundreds of miles from the research stations. The simians would not find living there so easy as Bretlia. They might even become more fierce on their new home world. They could adapt and learn to survive in their new home or die in the attempt. One thing was for sure, the Tretret and Amdor's whose blood was used to lure them into the boxes would not be forgotten. Wendy was returned to Bretlia to be with her family with the assurance those things in the trees would not scare her anymore. The council reasoned that by moving the simians to Terra they might have improved their lives. The simians were predators. On Bretlia they were top of the food chain and had no predators to hunt them. Their lives would have become complacent and lazy. On Terra they had to hunt with the knowledge they were being hunted. The dense higher branches would be their new homes. Flying creatures sought a new food source and on the ground hunting for food was a dangerous time. Even in the branches they were not completely safe. Snakes and giant poisonous insects would keep them constantly alert. They no longer moved as one or two anywhere. The simians always moved in groups with outer members looking and listening.

A Little Time Reminiscing

ALINA WAS WALKING on deck eighteen near section eighty five and was thinking how much she had learned, seen and experienced since being Captain. Met the Orions and Sorians among a number of what she called 'memories I can do without' catagory. Definetly low points in her command. Apollo's eighteen, nineteen and twenty never flew but recovered remarkable evidence when they returned to earth such as twenty's EB Mona Lisa. A life form not found on the moon just like the Long Island didn't exist either. Mona Lisa was a drop in a bucket for the space program at that time. Very hush hush. Now the same people are sitting in classes with advisors from other worlds learning new things that maybe, maybe man would discover in another thirty thousand years without them. Edinburgh, Miami and a few other cities around the globe were advancing science and medicine in gargantuan leaps almost daily. There was a minor skirmish near her that the Lomgren settled with a few bites and clawing injuries. Alina was so lost in thought she did not know it happened until she walked into her Tretret wall. They had closed into a tight circle around her. Almost falling back she was caught by a massive arm and gently lifted back to her feet. William's team members were taking several life forms away from her. She did not give the matter another thought.

She thought about when Davis said he wanted to show her something that would change her life. Placing her hand on the podium certainly did that. Hundreds of other wordly populations knew about the Long Island and her Captain. The Planetary Council knew that she had the finest engineers and medical staff on her ship in the fleet. She, Davis and Tony had made friends with some of the most remarkable individuals anywhere in this galaxy or the next. As she walked on to deck twenty two she was met by Koriat crewmen. Tony was right about them she was not disappointed she brought them aboard. Danielle, Danella and Carin learned more about their human Captain's everyday. Loreena was still trying to figure out her Captain's moods and body language and Carin told her don't try. She was still learning herself. Alina turned to go into a section and the door would not open. She tried to overide with her command and it was refused. Her Tretret commander put his weight and strength into it and barely budged the door. Before Alina could ask what was wrong she and her team were on the bridge. William and some structural engineers were ordered to open it. On precaution she had medical staff in isolation suits standing by for entry.

When it was opened they were met by a small force of the same creatures William and his team had captured only minutes before. These had no intention of being captured. They were not a match for the ship's entry team and the skirmish, if that, was a short one. Danielle had gone down to see who this intruder was and did not recognize them but the Lomgren recognized their smell immediately. Finding out how surgically altered Orion got aboard, again, undetected was a job for William and his team. The Tarnet command ship was hurtling toward the Long Island to take their favorite guests aboard their ship. The Koriat met the Orions for the first time and they were not impressed. Messages from the New Iberia and the Lincoln were the same. How did they get aboard and who is helping the Orion? It was not a member of the council. Another unknown enemy with a grudge against the council, or more likely, the Long Island. What was obvious is this unknown did not want to be connected to the Orions and face the council fleet. Safer to command from the shadows than face direct retribution. Interrogation by the Medusans revealed very little. The Orion's benefactor preferred being anonymous even to them. Since Davis was the first Captain of the Long Island he tried to think of who might hold a grudge against him and lost count after a few minutes of reflection. He was forced to consider that the attacks on the Long Island were not directed at Alina at all but at him.

The prisons on many worlds held those who were his enemies and would jump at the chance to help any planet eliminate him. The New Iberia was a war prize. They did not know of the standing order to prevent the ships cature by going into a core jump and kill everyone and everything on board including them. Alina and Davis shared a common trouble. Reminiscing was giving them a headache.

Settling Old Business

T HE TARNET COMMAND ship had graciously taken the Orion off the Captain's hands. This was not a reprieve for them anymore than it was for those who came before them. Some would make it to the Tarnet homeworld prisons however some would not. Prison on Tarnet or not survive a few more hours was dependent on the Tarnet Commnader's benevolence toward them. The Commander decided that the prisons were much worse than dying and the Orion's fates were sealed in a moment's contemplation.

The Orions were no longer aboard and section four was cleaned and empty ready for what ever new guests would come it's way. The Helium three reserves were near ninety one percent on all three ships respectively. Stores and supplies were brought aboard, checked and stored in their places. Engine output on all three ships was at peak levels and weapons were ready if the Captain so commanded. All battlecraft and scout ships were ready for mission capability. Boarding crews were selected and prepared at the Captain's command to engage any enemy they directed them against. By now, after Alina's report on the boarding and intruder skirmishes, Koriat's were now aboard the New Iberia as crew members as well. At a dinner of the three Captain's aboard the Lincoln all recieved reports that their respective ships were at full readiness and fully operational in all sections. Situation reports were clear with no incidents or calls for assistance. The boards were clear.

A comment was made about just trying a new start of things. All that they had been through was behind them. The unknown was a gaping question in front of them and there were so many wonders yet to see and discover. The research teams om Terra and Atlantis had found a workable symbiant balance and they were doing much better. The symians were surviving in great numbers on Terra the experiment with them was proving successful. Bretlian colonies were flourishing without the symians and Wendy was a happy young girl. That meant more than anything else to Alina. There were things that needed to be done before a new start could really be made. All three Captain's seemed to be thinking the same thing. On earth's scanners the Long Island, New Iberia and the Lincoln showed they were in geosynchronous orbit over the Captain's respective home towns. Sherman, Texas had not changed much as a result of the incidents there. Her mother was in absolutely great health and so happy to see her. Alina's family was still not sure who this woman was their mother was so thrilled to be with. And the giant creatures with her were forbodding and showed no emotion at all. There were these really odd dogs with her and Alina's aunt fainted when one said hello to her.

A Centaur remained on the outer perimeter with another of the dogs. These very tall and handsome men with some type of staff with a blade kept very close to this strange woman. Their mother accepted these creatures like they were old friends. The Koriats were very strange looking and none there would approach them. This strange woman called them over to her and introduced her mother to them. Her family looked up and saw several winged creatures flying above them. Police started to show up and they were immediately aware there were new members of the community present. An enormous wall of a creature blocked their way. A wave of a woman's hand with them and they were escorted forward. A sergeant that was there was worried how this report was going to sound to her superiors.

A creature the sergeant had no clue of what it was told her it was aware she was recording everything. One of the dogs told her to sit opposite the Captain and her leg's almost went out from under her. There was a forceful double clunk and looking saw the Centaur's front hooves on a patrol car's hood. The sergeant's stomach was really feeling uneasy. One of the flying creatures landed on the car's roof it's weapon close to the deputy's head. Once more this strange woman waved her hand and all of them backed off. The elderly woman they knew as Mrs. Grant was completely unaffected by all this commotion. As the woman got up to leave she gave their mother a hug and a kiss on the cheek and in a flicker of light she and the creatures were gone. Aboard the Long Island once more Danielle had the coordinates of the Lunar City laid in and ready for the Captain's order to enable.

In New Iberia, Louisiana Captain Davis in normal clothing was walking land his family had owned for generations. The Parish sheriff feeling cocky and going to read this stranger the riot act about trespassing was brought up short by a dog that blocked his way and warned him if he was a threat to the Captain he would die before he took three steps. Turning around a Centaur blocked his way. Turning his head to the right a giant stood between him and the stranger and on his other side a tall man with a blade of some type laid against his chest blocked his escape. The stranger told them to leave him alone and at that point the deputy felt wisdom was the better choice in talking to the stranger. The stranger knew alot about the area and the people who lived here. Asking if this family or that still lived here in New Iberia. Was the old high school still standing? There was something about the stranger that was so familiar he could not put his finger on. He knew this stranger. That was confirmed when the stranger asked how his wife Pam and his son were doing. If his son Mark was still ill he knew a doctor that could help him. In fact the doctor was part of his party.

Turning to him he blurted out, "Who are you?" "It's ok Paul, we went to school together. I've known you and your family since junior high." Paul's wife saw her husband's car on the Davis's land and pulled over to see what was going on. Mark was in the car as his health did not let him be alone. "Paul, are you OK?" The stranger's eyes lit up at seeing her and said "Hi Pam." Taken back for a moment at this strange man knowing her name she wasn't sure what to do. Instinctively she looked behind her in the car and the stranger asked if Mark was in the car. Fear started to show in her eyes and he said it was ok. He had a doctor in his party that could help Mark. Recognition flooded her eyes and she knew it was Mike Davis standing before her. "He is so sick Mike and there is no treatment for him. They give us a few months and we will lose him." Her voice broke and it took a little time for her to recover. "Pam the doctor with me can help Mark. Let him at least look at him." She shook her head yes and the doctor went to the car. "Captain I can help him but I have to have him in medical bay." Pam looked at him and said "Captain?" "Perhaps the two of you have heard of the advisors from other worlds in cities around the globe. I command the starship New Iberia in geosynchronous orbit above New Iberia as we speak. My medical team has technology thousands of years ahead earth medicine even at the current level. We can transport the three of you aboard my ship to the medical bay." "It would take month's to plan that type of flight." Pam said.

Mike snapped his fingers and they were aboard the New Iberia. Paul started to reach for his weapon and an enormous hand enveloped his entire lower arm. Mark was lying on a gurney and instruments they had never seen were giving readings on Mark's condition. Looking to see what was holding his arm a stern face towering over him glared at him shaking it's head warning him to not do that. "Captain, "the doctor was saying," we need to act now if we are to save this child." Pam shook her head yes and the medical team swarmed around Mark. "Danella walked up to them and said, "I am Danella, the Captain's second in command.The doctors and nurses will be busy for a while and we will call you when the procedure is complete. Let me show you some of the things we have aboard." Pam wanted to stay with Mark and the Captain approved her request. In the meantime there was no reason some of the ships wonders couldn't say hello to her.

She asked for some coffee or water and both was brought to her by a Centaur. A Lomgren told her that her son would be good as new and not to worry. She heard a voice above her and a winged creature was hovering above her and reassuring her that all would be good. A tug on her arm she looked down to see a small creature trying to tell her something in clicks and tones. Loreena said, "She said it will be ok. I am Loreena, the Captain's communications officer. If you need something let me know." One after another these wonderous creatures would come to speak to her. Before she knew the time had passed the doctor stood in front of her and said everything went well and there were no complications during the procedure. She could see her son now. Mark was talking a mile a minute and smiling for the first time since he was a toddler. The Captain and Paul came into the medical bay and when Mark saw his dad his arms opened wide and he was laughing. Pam was so overcome with emotion there was a medic next to her in case she had a problem with all around her. Loreena walked up to Paul and said they found his patrol car abandoned, his wife's car empty and no trace of either of them. A search had been started to locate him. Every municipal, county, state and federal law enforcement agency in the immediate area were involved. Missing police officers tended to cause more than a little concern.

Pam and Mark would be aboard about two more days. The New Iberia would remain in orbit for that time. Explaining to the sheriff what happened would take some time. In case he needed help the Captain would send a Treverig that specialized in law to go down with him. Might ease the doubt factor. The day that Pam and Mark materialized back in their home she took her son to the doctor's office. The doctor and his staff were stunned with the change in Mark. A child near the end of life a few short days ago is now a healthy, vibrant, active child.

Tony stood in the living room of his house in Houston. How many years had it been since he was here and realized it had been a matter of months at best since he stood here last. Dust covered everything. The Cerollon were happily munching on the spiders that had seemed to take over the house since he left. One of the Lomgren suddenly blocked his way and was looking in a back corner of the kitchen. When Tony looked closer a Diamondback rattlesnake was curled up and ready to strike. A Strefdan with him struck out with his blade severing the snake in two pieces. Tony told him that the head was still dangerous because the fangs had venom in them. A Centaur smashed the head with his hooves. Another was found in the back porch but this time a Koriat moved so quickly the snake was caught mid strike and killed by crushing it in his hands. The snake tried to turn it's head to strike this enemy and failed. Scorpions were everywhere and who knew how many more snakes had taken up residence in the house since his absence. This house was now a death trap for anyone entering it. Much as he hated to do it when he and his surface team left the house there was a flicker of the sun's light and the house ceased to exist. His home was a ship in orbit and the responsibilities of a Captain shaped who he had become. There were other pressing duties to attend to right now and when he was back on his ship ordered it to Lunar City orbit. The New Iberia would already be there waiting for him.

Alina and her surface team were prepared to walk on the lunar surface. In what had become standard procedure any stones near the cemetery were removed before the Captain ever set foot on the surface. Larger rocks that had moved close to the cemetery were destroyed. William's team had shields with them to deflect any stones that flew to close the Captain. Alina was walking among the headstones whose numbers had a habit of always increasing as did the memories of those laid to rest here. The sound of rocks impacting the shields had become so common she longer really heard them anymore. She was bending down to brush the dust from a nameplate when she was grabbed and snatched away. Held in the arms of a Tretret she saw a stone that was walking searching for her. A hand swiped it up and threw it far away effortlessly. Ever since Apollo's eighteen, nineteen and twenty missions the rocks had found human blood a delicacy. The argument that rocks were not a life form didn't hold water. NASA and the world's space exploration agencies would one day discover life forms far more amazing than these living moon rocks. How life is or is not defined depends on what planet you are on at the time.

The Tarnet Commander reported being attacked by an unknown enemy in sector David Four a few days past. The ship signature was very similar to that of the ship that left the Long Island disabled. They were not able to escape this time and a long battle ended in the enemy being destroyed. No answer as to why the attack or who they were just the final result of it. Several of his crew had been killed and they were on the way to the cemetery to lay them to rest. Alina never thought this place would become the giant place it was. The grave's numbers grew ever closer to the Lunar City itself and maybe at some time be on both ends of it. There were no remains of the enemy. A self destruct on their ship made certain there was no way to identify them. Another door closed in her journey as Captain. If she could have seen herself before her experience in the shuttle she doubted she would know who that strange woman was. Aboard her ship once more she entered the bridge to the now familiar "Captain is on the bridge". Danielle reported the ship was fully operational and ready for the next destination. Alina was quiet for a few moments then said to set course for Sam One.

Tony entered his bridge and was informed that his ship was scheduled for docking to make addtions to it. "What type of additions?" he asked. "Captain, the ship will double in size and width, new weapons systems will be installed, there will be crew additions and changes in the engines based on what we have discovered on the Constellation will give it greater speed." Pointing at Carin he said, "Remind the council I decide on any additions to my ship including crew members not them." Hesitating for a moment not sure what to do since the orders came from the council itself. Looking at her he said, "Send it now." Using the channel designated for the ship's seconds Carin told Danielle and Danella what happened. Both said the Captain made those decisions. The council could not override his authority. As long as she was aboard her loyalty was to her Captain. If she had trouble understanding that there were plenty of others waiting in line to take her place at a moment's notice that did not. Maybe there was something wrong with her processor what ever the reason she felt she could no longer do her duties aboard the Lincoln. The next morning there was a new second in command on the bridge. "Good morning Captain, I am Ellyssa your new second in command." "Where is Carin?" Why is she not here?" "She was deactivated Captain. There were conflicts in her programming. I was given all of her memories and command codes." "All of her memories? Essentially you are Carin in that respect am I right?" "Essentially Captain, yes. But I still have my own self awareness."

Tony asked Alina and Mike to send Danielle and Danella to brief Ellyssa on her responsibilities. This change of second in command without his authorization did not sit well with Tony and the light would shine in their meager little minds that he was the Captain of the Lincoln and made these decisions. Turning to his new second he asked "Ellyssa, where is Carin right now?" "Captain her form is in storage on deck nine, section eleven." "Have engineering meet me on deck nine, section eleven in four minutes." Engineering was waiting when he arrived. He told them to reactivate Carin and repair her if they could. First he wanted to know why she chose to be deactivated. "Captain", she said, "I could no longer function as I should have and deactivation was my program's solution. Why did you reactivate me Captain?" "Engineering can repair your programming conflicts and return you to duty. I can only have one second in command so you will be third in command. As to why I reactivated you call it respect or admiriation for you as a person. Ellyssa will need help adjusting to my command style. I will need you to help out there." Entering the bridge Tony told Loreena to send urgent to the council. "Carin would be reactivated as third in command. If they disagree with my decision remind them I am in command." Turning to Ellyssa he said, "You are my second in command and I expect you to fulfill those duties. I know you have Carin's memories but you do not have her experience. Carin will be here to call on and help you do your job."

Danielle and Danella were not sure what to make of this situation on the Lincoln. Third in command was not a place they were familiar with. A message from Tony clarified that Ellyssa was his second and Carin was his third in command and still authorized to use second in command channel. Carin was confused by her human Captain before. That he would reactivate her because of his respect or admiration for her as a person was a brand new concept to her. Confusion as to loyalty was no longer an issue for her. Her loyalty was and would be to her Captain no matter the council's directives. Any other Captain treated their androids as machines. The human Captain's treated them as individuals not machines. "Ellyssa. how long are these additions to the ship supposed to take?" "Additions to the ship Captain? I am not aware of additions to the ship being made." Carin came onto the bridge. "Captain the additions were to take three weeks of round the clock work. Fifty additions to the crew are proposed but their approval depends on your decision." "Welcome back Carin." "Glad to be back Captain." Carin filled Ellyssa in on the additions to the ships proposal. The Captain still had to decide if they happened or not. As a side thought Tony told both of them they were a team not competitors. The Captain and Loreena were talking quietly. When Ellyssa started to walk over to them Carin touched her arm and shook her head no. As they finished the Captain called both of them over to join the conversation.

It continued for another twenty minutes before a distress call from the Volitny ship came in. They were several light years away and the Captain ordered jump capabilty in engines. Time to intercept was eight minutes at jump speed. Weapons were brought on line and Carin had two battlecraft manned and ready for deployment. Medical bay was put on alert. Ellyssa did not know what was going on but Carin seemed to have everything well in hand. Turning to her Carin said, "I have been through many of these with the Captain before and know his procedures and commands before he gives them. You will learn. Danielle and Danella helped me enormously to understand the Captain and he still surprises me everyday with some new part of himself being revealed." Ellyssa said, "I have all your memories but have no idea what is going on. Why?" "Mnenomic patterns for experience does not go to memory patterns. It is in a completely different processor you have but have not activated yet. The engineers can activate it and transfer the patterns I have to your processor. Everything will make perfect sense after they do."

Carin commanded that the scanners look for the Volitny ship and when located check for life signs. It was found adrift with minimal life support remaining. The battle craft were deployed and those not critically injured were taken back to the Lincoln. Critically injured were transported directly to the medical bay. Additional battlecraft and scout ships were deployed around the Volitny ship to protect it. Less critically injured were in triage areas set up on deck three, hangar bay one and treated there. Ellyssa was returning after her processor had been downloaded and was now up to date on all aspects. Ships to tow the Volitny ship back to it's homeworld for repairs were on the way. The presence of the Lincoln stopped the attack and their attackers fled from the battle. The space around the Lincoln was soon filled with council ships arriving to assist. The Long Island and the New Iberia were arriving on the scene. The Long Island would take the only damaged enemy ship aboard and tear it apart. Danielle ordered a boarding party standby when it was opened. Sealed off by isolation shields the boarding crew entered cautiously. Several dead of an unfamiliar life form were strewn about the control room. Continuing both directions The Lomgren were smelling the air for everything and listening for any movement that might be trouble. They were able to access all but one section.

For some reason the Centaurs were nervous when they neared it. Tretrets and Strefden were right beside them. Lomgren were right under them ready to deal with what ever was there. Koriats were next to the door on either side of it. The sound of the door being activated from inside brought all to readinesss. Small creatures like children started coming out. There was a commotion to close the door and the Centaur in front charged through the door. The sound of a battle and the Longren hurtled past the others into the compartment. Screaming brought the rest through the opening and into a nightmarish picture. Creatures, chidren maybe hung from rafters were all over. The rage in the boarding team hit fever level and no mercy was shown those there. Medics were brought in and it would be a long time before any thing would be known. What was clear was the ones they killed were traffickers in humans or any thing that paid them well. Of those in the first section still alive the Medusan was able to learn that children regardless of planetary origin were big money items.

Alina's rage was greater than Danielle had ever seen it before. The Tarnet Commander offered to take them before William killed them in some horrible manner. From death in some horrible manner to the worst prison that the Tarnet could concieve. No trial was necessary to send them there. Tarnet justice was different than on many worlds. Prison in a place that never got below one hunfred Reloigh or one that never got above minus three Reloigh. There was a mining prison in the jungle sections of the planet that was guarded by creatures that stayed near the walls to sting and torture any hapless victim that might try to escape. The Tarnet Commander had so many decisions to choose from.

Alina didn't care what the Medusans had to do but she wanted the planetary origin of these animals. The weapons systems were not terribly powerful but useful in an ambush. The Volitny were not looking for them so the cloaking devices hid them until the attack. The Volitny dead were taken to the Lunar City cemetery and laid to rest there. The search for the planet of origin of the attackers continues. The prisoners took their own lives leaving only their bodies as evidence of their existence. The human Captain's ships were joined by many others of the council protecting the damaged Volitny ship. Tarnet worked alongside Bolterer, Cantenerran, Traverig, and Strefden as one team. Dofgrara worked with Sinefor, Amdor and Bretlian in any capacity they could. Bretlia was admitted to the council on word of the Tarnet Commander. So far their service was equal to any crew member. Wendy was growing so fast. Occasionally she would ask about Alina and where she was.

A message from the Prime Minister was transmitted to the Long Island. England was prospering as it had never done before. Scotland was a mecca of advanced sciences. Ireland was getting the benefits of the advisors presence and even taught a few of them how to drink Irish ales and whiskys. "When Ireland Calls" or "The Isle of Innisfree" just doesn't sound quite right in the Volitny language. The advisors were fascinated that so many countries whose borders are so close can speak a different language and have different cultures side by side. Britain's English is not like Gaelic anymore than French is like German or the classical Spanish of Spain. India has over four hundred dialects within it's borders and the Polish language is not like Lithuania's. Humans, as the advisors continued to learn, were totally unpredictable and their actions very difficult to understand. Well, they would admit, most of the time humans made no sense at all. How this primitive life form survived all this time was a mystery to them. A line on a map seperated them. It may as well have been an impenetrable wall of Corium seperating them from the others about them. The United Nations was an unfathomable entity. The advisors could spend a hundred years here studying humans and earth's governments and never come up with a logical reason for either.

The three human Captains were unlike any of their planetary kind. Entrusted with their ships and crews they seemed to have risen above their planetary origins. The Long Island and the New Iberia had formed their own legends mainly in no small part because of their Captain's. The Illinois Lincoln was becoming better known but there were still council member planets that knew nothing of the ship or her human Captain. Carin and Ellyssa were working very smoothly as a team and they were proving there was a place for a third in command position to the point the Long Island and New Iberia were considering the change on a trial basis. The Tretrets assigned to Carin before were still her security team. Tony made the surface party change that since he had a third in command either Elyssa or Carin would accompany him in his landing party. One would always remain aboard as acting Captain. Carin spent little time on the bridge as she was acting in the Captain's behalf putting out minor personnel skirmishes and disagreements. Seeing to it that his orders were being followed, commanded a boarding party force, investigated reports of violence against any crew member and had the authority to send the aggressor to section four on her command alone. An Orion was discovered hidden in the food supply section and taken to section four. Tony sent Ellyssa and Carin to deal with this new breach. A Tarnet ship was four hundred thousand kilometers from the Lincoln and arrived in time to be part of an inquiry held at the Captain's order. Brian had members of his team testing the food section for contaminates or toxins. The Long Island and the New Iberia were not enroute to the Lincoln but were following events through Danielle's and Danella's reports.

Lomgren were sent through every hall, accessway and corner of the section searching for additional unwanted passengers and found none. Cerollons flew into the upper reaches of the section and looked into every possible hiding place or darkend space finding nothing in their sweeps. Drones programmed to detect life forms and all known explosive or incendiary type of weapon flew continous patrols back and forth and in random patterns throughout the section. The only possible conclusion was that a crew member or members helped it get aboard and presumably if not caught to escape. The task of finding this individual or individuals fell on Brian's shoulders. He would not fail in his search. He reported directly to Ellyssa and when found she would determine what happened to them.

Reports of anomallies or anything out of order no matter how small were investigated promptly. Centaurs and Lomgren patrolled together. Both were ready and capable of killing what ever they encountered. Koriats and Strefden patrolled with Tretret or part of Brian's team leaving nothing unturned. Battlecraft were manned and sealed to prevent someone or something from using them to get off the ship. The Orion took his own life so he would not be saying anything to anyone. An autopsy may or not reveal something but the Captain was not leaving any avenue unexplored. He wanted answers as to how the Orion got aboard undetected.

Time passed with no new information on the Orion incident. Brian had failed to discover the agent or agents involved in the case. He would not give up and if his power cells expired before succeeding his replacement would take up where Brian left off. Time, to an android, does not exist. Times of activation and deactivation are the only parameters they deal with. Hit and miss incidents continued to occur with the lifeform responsible for the disabling of the Long Island. But the crew learned with every encounter and was better prepared than the last time they fought. Staerr advised Danielle the ship was closing on the Long Island and then stopped. It held station about three thousand kilometers off the starboard side for awhile evidently thinking this one through. The wormhole formed behind it and it retreated before engaging. Long distance scans showed the Long Island the only ship in eight million kilometers at any direction. Alina had William and his team scan all decks for lifeforms aboard that did not belong just in case the enemy tried to transport a team on to the Long Island during the standoff. Scan result was negative on all decks. The unknown enemy had never encountered a human Captain before. These things were very unpredictable and unstable for their purposes.

Terra Two Chaos

REPORTS FROM THE Terra Two research station were over riding and jibberish to Captain Davis. Tanya and the Defgrara worked to sort out the chaotic communications. By Jump speed measurement the New Iberia was three hours away. The Planetary Council was always looking for new members to strengthen the council's position. Two new planets had joined, one which was the Fremlorian world had a ship in Terra Two orbit when the New Iberia arrived on scene. The Lincoln even at jump speed was more than a full day off. The Long Island arrived within an hour of the New Iberia. In a playful anger Alina demanded to know what they did to her planet. Most of the ships Captain's did not know Alina well enough to tell sarcasm from real anger. Davis told her to be quiet while he figured things out. Most of the research team members were already transported aboard the orbiting council ships. There were some notable absences among those still on the surface. Dr. Anlon Trevity of the Tarnet Planetary Research Facility was one such absence. Dr. Croita Drevce of the Volitny Deep Space Research Foundation was another. Knowing the Tarnet and Volitny crews they would exhaust eveey man in the recovery of their teams. The Volitny had another ship enroute to Terra to assist in locating Dr. Drevce no matter the risk encountered. Davis had a planet wide scan done to determine the stability of the planet below them.

There were a few geologic anomallies but nothing significant close to the research facility. The presence of the simians were noted in mass only a few kilometers away. The balance of life forms were still as previously noted with increasing numbers closing in on the facility. Biologists did note signs of extreme anxiety in the smaller dinosaurs and it was spreading to the larger ones. Old timers of the security teams on the surface, those that had survived more than twenty days, led the Tarnet and Volitny rescue teams deep into the planets forest. The presence of the simians were becoming an increasing danger as they moved deeper and deeper into the undergrowth. Several Lomgren because of their acute senses were included in the rescue parties. An attempted ambush of the rescue parties failed because the Lomgren knew where the simians were before they could close around them. The old timers had learned to use other native animals on the planet against another and this helped cause the demise of many simian attackers. There was a foul stench as they approached a clearing and a security team agent pushed a Tarnet officer away from a worm that rose from the ground trying to swallow it whole.

The agent did not seem to be too surprised at the worm's attack and continued on into the trees without a second thought about it. The simians that did not flee from this melee were no match for the rescue team's weapons. Eventually those remaining joined their fellows in retreat. Larger numbers of animals were closing on the facility and the researchers did not know why. Samples of the air were taken and analyzed with no usable information revealed as to the odd behavior of the animals. More confusing than their actions was that as they entered the compound they began to settle down showing less and less anxiety. Soon the number of animals were in the hundreds inside the compound. They sensed something because those near the compounds inner fence perimeters were constantly sniffing the air. How would animals that had never seen a fence before know that they were safe inside it? One researcher on the Volitny ship made an offhand comment of "Mystery numer eighteen thousand three hundred and four. Animals react unpredictably showing amazing intelligence. Why?"

Aboard the New Iberia where the senior most researchers were tansported to discuss these events some were having a problem dealing with crew members. Physicists were not sure what to make of cats discussing quantum physics equations with them. Biochemists the top of their fields on earth were being taken to school by crew members that looked like half semi human and half something else. A few individuals that had pretty high opinions of themselves were being taught by creatures that looked like Centaurs. Star navigation specialists were showing the leaders in Astronomy and planetary science specialists on earth the most rudimentary navigation rules for deep space pilots and none of them could follow their instructors. They could not understand the concept of the science behind it. Physicians and surgeons rescued from Terra were in the medical bay and the doctors were talking about concepts humanity had not even considered as plausible like it was aincent history, first semester pre-med course requirements. The medical stations were so advanced the doctors were incapable of operating them. Security team members that were not slouches by any measurement were getting their butts thrown about the landing bay by a creature not even five feet tall and a female at that like they were toys. Danella feeling bad for the team finally introduced their opponent as a Koriat warrior. This did little to soothe their bruises and wounded egos. Those still on the surface discovered the remains of those they were seeking.

Scans on the ship showed the animals in the compound would not go beyond the inner fence perimeter setting neither wing or claw outside the boundry. How did they know they were safe in the compound and what understanding did they possess that the researchers had missed completely in assessing their intelligence? Mystery eighteen thousand three hundred and five. As evening darkened the skies there was a change. Whatever the animals sensed had apparently gone away and they left the compound disappearing into the countryside. In a matter of minutes none of the animals remained in the compound. The droppings they left behind would be destroyed by the New Iberia's weapons focused to a fine degree limiting area affected by the blast. The longer the researchers stayed on Terra and Atlantis the more they realized the ignorance they possessed about these worlds and the animals in them. Did the dinosaurs on earth over sixty five million years ago have this intelligence or was this trait exclusive to these animals alone? That question could never be answered.

The situation on the planets below seemed to be resolved but Captain Davis did not allow himself such optimism. Continuous scans from the ship as well as battlecraft flying the planets surface testing for radiation levels, unknown gases in the air,magnetic field anomallies and samplings of the water sources on the planet were being checked in minute detail. Captain Davis did not like chaos in his sector and this incident on Terra certainly qualified in his eyes as being that. He had remained on the bridge for almost eighteen hours straight and showed no intent of retiring for the night. Danella watched him closely ready to implement any orders he may have at his discretion. He turned to Tanya and told her she was third in command and would be given authority to use the channel for seconds. A new android was activated and sent to the bridge. Sandra was the name given her by Captain Davis and she took over Tanya's responsibilites. Tanya was sent to the Terran surface with a security team landing party. As soon as the Tretret and Lomgren materialized on the surface they were instantly alert to someone or something near them. Tanya's safety was their responsibilty and they would die protecting her. Closing around her they looked in every direction seeking this presence that did not want to be found. The Cerollon shot skyward and tried to see anything that didn't belong. Even they knew something was not right and were skittish at any noise or movement.

The Strefden, Centaurs and Koriats were ready for anything that came close but their unknown guest refused to show itself. The massive arms of the Tretret covered Tanya almost completely. Holding onto one of their arm's she moved forward. For once Tanya was beginning to understand how Captain Grant must feel surrounded by this formidible wall. A Lomgran deliberately bumped Tanya behind a Tretret and froze looking in the direction of a darkend building. Snarling with teeth bared and fangs dripping venom he remained still locked on his target. A Centaur with a Koriat closed on the building and then heard something moving inside. They froze trying to locate where it was going. Cerollons were circling overhead watching those below them ready to attack from above. Watching the Lomgran's gaze Strefden moved quietly along the front edge of the building and then they too heard something inside going from place to place not remaining anywhere more than a few seconds.

On the New Iberia and Long Island both Captains followed the surface team activities as closely as possible. The Lincoln was only now in range of Terra and would remain in orbit on station where Captain Davis would need them most. Tony sent Brian down to the surface with Tanya's team. As an android Brian had special abilities including heat sensors that enabled him to locate life forms from body heat signatures. As he scanned the buildings interior he was picking several reptilian lifeforms. There were more on an upper level though a diferent signature than those close by them. He told a Tretret there was one trying to come behind him very quietly. Turning he saw what could have been a velociraptor on earth but did not look like one he had seen on computer screen briefings. This giant in front of it could feed several of them for a long time. It was huge but a Tretret is not slow or defenseless. A sudden attack resulted in it being thrown into a second raptor.

A second attack was immediate and a bite on the back of one raptor's neck proved fatal in matter of seconds. The dinosaurs tried to get all this food in a single place to make killing easier. Cerollons, embroiled in their own aerial battles for survival, were unable to help those below them. These victims were not going to die easily nor did they show any fear.

Several Strefden made it to the second level and were immersed in knashing teeth and tails that were meant to knock them over. Blades sung in the air as they flashed in the light of the approaching morning. Howls of pain as tails and claws were severed in a single stroke drove some out of the building to rush into the team surrounding Tanya where they fared no better. Koriat blades sunk deep into raptor flesh diminishing their numbers rapidly. Centaurs used their hooves to stomp and kick unfortunate victims to death. Smaller animals learned that a Centaur's rear kicks are as devastating as the fronts crushing power. Much larger animals moved into the battle arena and began to feed on those felled in battle. An easy meal is hard to come by and there was a bounty here. The errant Pterodactyl or what ever they were called on this accursed planet would sometimes fall into a larger animal feeding and become a side dish for the taking. The surface team backed out of the building leaving those there to work out their own survival. A Centaur held a Lomgran in his arms as they backed out. Transported aboard the New Iberia medics were waiting for them to return. One took the Lomgran and rushed it to the medical bay.

When Captain Grant heard of the injured Lomgran she made a special trip to the New Iberia to be with it while it was being cared for. Many of the ship's crew members always marvelled at how these frail humans showed so much strength toward others and genuinely cared about them. It didn't matter what the crew member was the Captain's cared equally for them all. For most of the crews the lost times on the moon's surface for all the millenias multiplied by countless more by those that sent them was all but forgotten. If the civilizations that made them, sent them deep into space and then left them like used up trash could see them now. Messages mentioning Captain Grant's ship was assumed to mean the Long island. In fact it referred to the Constellation renamed Grant's Constrellation. It was being sent on it's first mission for the Planetary Council. A planet in the direct path of a star going nova had to get the entire planet's civilization removed and moved to a new home as quickly as possible. Grant's Constellation would be the ideal transport for the planet's inhabitants.

The loss would be the animal life forms left behind found nowhere else as far as the council knew within eight light years. As many of the different lifeforms as possible would be transported in stasis to the new planet so not all were lost. Placed in stasis the creatures would wake up on their new world unharmed for the travails in their relocation. How they adapted or did not adapt to their new home would take time to discover. Biologists and Zoologists from earth volunteered to accompany these animals to their new home. When would they would have another chance to take part in such a wonderous mission of mercy? This was a once in a lifetime opportunity. The annals of science on earth were filled with this scientist's or that one's efforts to save a single animal from extinction. These would be saving hundreds from extinction. Animals found nowhere else in a galaxy's realm and possibly never be seen again by human eyes. Every possible moment to gather as much information as they could on the voyage would have to be utilized. As important as the mission itself the payoff would be releasing them into their new home. To take part in the seeding of a planet with animals from another was science fiction before today. When the sun on the new home world rose new life would greet it's warming rays for the very first time. Lessons had been learned from Terra and the most important was life needed to be left alone to flourish and so it would be.

The victory of the animal seeding was balanced by the tragedy on Terra Two. Lives lost in every area of the research and security teams. The facility was a total loss now inhabited by the animals on the planet. The teams would return when a new facility was built and ready for occupancy by Planetary Council members not reptilian hunters. Captain Davis was watching the planet pass beneath his Captain's yacht as it flew a safe distance above the ground. Sheilds kept the gigantic flying animals and insects from being too comfortable aboard his yacht's hull. The planet started out as the most promising of all scientific explorations in Queen Three. It represented the greatest of failures not even taking a full day to be destroyed. The research facility would be rebuilt in another location on the planet and the lessons learned here would be reflected in the architectural designs. Tanya was aboard the New Iberia on the bridge as Captain Davis and Danella discussed all that had occured here and what changes should be made to prevent a repeat of this chaos. Sandra kept Tanya up to date on all communications and changes coming in from the council. As much as the council expressed it's desire something specific be done in a certain time frame Captain Davis was her Captain and her allegiance was to him.

Danielle and Staerr and Ellyssa and Carin had the same position. Regardless of the council's insistence about something their dedication was to their Captains. The Long Island and the Lincoln had left orbit and set course for World One Sam. Transporting down to her house it felt so good feeling the sun on her again. It was not long before the rejuvenating effect of the planet took it's hold on her. The gray highlights began to fade and replaced by the shimmering brunette tones of her normal hair color. Even Tony could feel some type of rejuvenation in himself the longer they stayed there. Captain Grant's Tretret commander told her that Captain Davis would be transporting down in a few hours. Something happened to make the animals enter the compound and remain there until something around them changed. Now the entire facility was inhabited by worms, six foot long beetles, millipedes over five feet long and weighing close to one hundred fifty pounds, prehistoric forms of crocodiles and he could not begin to guess what else was there. Monitors that were still operational in the higher elevations of the structures were filled with images of dragonflies and flying reptiles making new homes in their observation towers. And there was something else there in the dust. Humanoid footprints of some type. Bipedal and having six toes on each foot but the author of these prints was not to be seen anywhere. They were not from a simian. No mistaking those prints. These were from a human or humanoid creature. From the print's size it was a small creature weighing not more than one hundred five pounds or less.

Alina was relaxing with Mike and Tony when a little girl ran up to her and wrapped her in a squeezing hug. Wendy was so glad to see her and Alina was frankly taken back a little by her being there. Tony lifted his hand and said, "I am why she is here. Thought you might like to see her again." Wendy was talking a mile a minute and Alina could not get a word in edge wise. Mike was applauding Wendy. Alina looked at him not understanding. He said, "I never thought I would find anyone that talked as much as you do." She acted like she was going to backhand him and then laughed. Staerr transported down and Wendy rushed to her. She whispered something to her and Staerr said she could probably find some chocolate ice cream somewhere. Staerr walked over to the three Captains and reported on the small footprints seen in the dust on Terra Two. All three were speechless. How could a humanoid that small survive in a world like Terra Two? Mystery eighteen thousand three hundred and six. The scientists assigned to Terra Two were returned to their home planets to wide acclaim. The research station on Atlantis was going strong and yeilding information that could not be believed unless you were the scientists witnessing it. All the data they had collected wasn't a minute fraction of what they could have learned if they had been able to stay. As it was their careers were made and all published their version of what Terra was like.

What Is She Doing Now?

WHEN ALINA REBOARDED the Long Island something possessed her and she said, "Captain to bridge." "Danielle here Captain." "Danielle set condition three, get us out of here emergency, ready fifteen battlecraft at attack evade pattern. Deploy battlecraft. All hands battle stations." As she walked through the halls crew members were rushing to their battle assignments. She could hear the battlecraft being deployed when she walked by a hangar bay. Captain Davis was entering the bridge of the Newe Iberia hoping for a quiet day. It was about to be shattered. "Captain," Danella was saying, "the Long island has gone to Condition three, deployed fifteen battlecraft at attack evade pattern and set course and speed emergency protocol. The Lincoln has set intercept course and gone to Condition three as well. Her battlecraft are manned and ready to deploy." Captain Davis was thinking is there one day, just one day my little girl doesn't get into trouble. "Danella, set intercept course, Condition four until we know more and have three battlecraft manned and ready to deploy." Incoming messages from other council ships to the New Iberia were overlapping and wanting to know what their response was. Long Island was not responding to hails from their ships.

"Danella monitor the Long island's communications and keep me advised." "Aye, Captain. Monitor communications." Davis looked at Danella who indicated no communications were detected from the Long Island. "Danella, set Condition three, man all battle stations and ready two additional battlecraft. Weapons online and available my command." "What," he was asking himself, "is she doing now?" Tanya told the Captain five hours to intercept with the Long Island. Danella reported, "Still no communications from Long Island Captain." "Tanya," he said, "send distress codes to the other council ships in the Long Island's proximity. Stand by for enemy engagement." Turning to Danella he said, "I want two boarding teams readied. Hostile reception imminent." An enemy that tried to stop the council ships at this point would not survive the attempt.

"Captain," Danella was saying, "we are picking up indications of heavy fighting in the area of the Long Island. The Captain is in medical bay and Staerr is out of commission. Danielle is damaged but still in command. There are four damaged battlecraft with two more destroyed completely. Nine are still in the fight. Casualties on almost all decks are being reported."

The vengenance Captain Davis would bring to bear on this enemy was of a magnitude only a man protecting his family was capable of. Weapons were readied and at the first possible moment of engagement he let the enemy have every bit of his fury. Three enemy ships tried to destroy the New Iberia and found themselves in the weapons fire of the Tarnet command ship. The Volitny ship Pretorra locked two more enemy ships in her sights and destroyed them with a flash of light from her bow weapons. Davis and Tony boarded the Long Island and went straight to the medical bay. Alina was not concious and she looked frail and there were burns on her arms and face. Davis went to the bridge, placed his hand on the pedastel and said he was assuming command of the Long Island until Captain Grant was able to return. Staerr looked in a bad way but the engineers would start work on her right away. Danielle was damaged and Tony ordered Elyssa to assume her duties until she was able to on her own. Davis looked around and there were several Tretret lying dead where the Captain would have been moments before. Repeated impacts on the Long Island's hull reminded him the battle was not over. The Long Island, due to her size, moved slower than the New Iberia but she was not a tortise by any measure.

Elyssa wore the uniform of the second in command. Her orders were accepted and followed with out question. Another battlecraft was destroyed and Captain Davis felt their loss as much as Captain Grant would. The Long Island had weapons, again because of her size, smaller council ships did not possess including the New Iberia and the Lincoln. These weapons Captain Davis remembered and ordered ready for firing. Other council ships backed off before the weapons were used. In a matter of seconds every ship, meteor, comet and particle of space dust within eight hundred thousand kilometers in front of the Long Island ceased to exist.Enemy ships trying to escape were destroyed with out mercy or consideration they were running away. Rescue ships were dispatched to bring back the crews of the damaged vessels and any enemy, unless some survived to flee, died in the coldness of space. His little girl was lying in the medical bay severly injured but alive because of the Tretret that defended her with their lives. He reminded himself how often he took their protective shield for granted. He would never do so again. He and Tony were waiting for the doctor to come out and give them a report on how she was doing. The Tretret with her started to leave having been thrown out by the doctor and Tony ordered them back to Alina's side and not to leave her unprotected at any time. In tones evoking the wrath of the Tarnet god Trelee he ordered the doctors to work around the Tretret. They were not leaving her side.

The Tarnet commander had just transported aboard and was standing there when Tony threatened the doctors. He was laughing but stopped when he saw Alina. His normally crystal eyes were turning dark when he saw what the enemy had done to her. "Please tell me," he was telling the human Captain's. "the Orion's are responsible for this attack." "Commander Triro we don't know who or what the enemy was. We do know that many of our crew members were lost. Danielle was damaged and Staerr is out of commission. The engineers are trying to repair and reactivate her." Danielle and Staerr damaged. That was hard to swallow. Yes, they were androids but they had become so much more than that to the Tarnet. They were friends and compatriots, damn near family to them. The engineers sent reports that the injuries that Danielle and Staerr recieved were from defending the Captain. Now that made sense. Tanya was sent by Captain Davis to the Long island to help Elyssa. When she could not leave the bridge Tanya would handle what ever arose. Wearing the uniform of the third in command, with Captain Davis on the New Iberia, she was second in command and her security team was always present.

Captain Davis was standing at the entrance of the treatment suite where Alina was with Commander Triro. Her life signs were weak and the doctors were very concerned. The fact that Captain Davis already assumed command in the event Captain Grant passed away the ship would go on. The enemy was not known and the reason they attcked was not known. Danielle was able to inform Captain Davis that the Captain unexpectedly ordered the ship to Condition three and the fifteen battle craft deployed. Emergency protocols were implemented in getting the ship out of the area. The fact that the battle craft were ordered to attack evasive kept them from being destroyed outright in the battle. Still, with all the precautions, the Captain was injured. Her Tretret and Strefden refused to budge and stood between her and the weapons blasts giving their lives for her. The Long Island would set course for the Lunar City once more hopefully not to bury her too this time. Messages sent by Danella to the Prime Minister of England of the Captain's severe injuries were returned with a request to be with her when they were close enough to transport him aboard. His security team was used to transporting from London to orbital space in the wink of an eye. They hoped their duty here did not end up in being the Captain's pallbearers to a cold lonely grave on the moon's surface.

Art work donated by the Captain to the British Museum of Art were still being studied. The paints used were of no known composition familiar to humanity. The images were a mystery. Are they of creatures and landscapes on other planets or an example of their version of earth's artist Picasso? The books from the Lunar City building's library were not translated yet because there was no earth language that could be used as a key to translate them. The advisors were unable to assist because their languages formed long after this civilization was flourishing. Alina remained non responsive in the medical bay. She would not be there to honor the dead this time. Representatives of the Planetary Council arrived in a steady flow to pay their respects to the Captain while they still could. Despite the advanced medicine and equipment her condition was not improving. Perhaps prematurely Danella sent a message to Alina's mother of her severe injuries and failure to respond to treatment so far. Her condition was stable but very guarded. Her mother that had seemed so happy and changed was now crying almost constantly. Her family did not know why. Despite all attempts on the part of her family she could not be consoled. She kept looking up at the moon wringing her hands in panic and desperation because there was nothing she could do. Captain Davis made the decision to transport her mother to Alina's side. One moment their mother was there and the next she was gone not to be seen anywhere.

Tanya escorted her mother to the medical bay from the transport pad and left her in the care of the medics attending her daughter. Attempts to call their mother's cell phone merely said there was no service available. A bed was brought in and placed next to Alina's bed so she could be near her. Food was brought to her so she could always be next to her daughter. These amazing doctors had saved her life and now was fighting to save her daughter. After a full day had passed on earth and no contact with their mother seeming any time soon a missing persons report was filed with the Sherman, Texas police. Tony remembered World One Sam and the effect the planet had on humans in particular. He had no idea if it would help her but was worth a try.Tony on the Long Island ordered the ship sent to Sam and at maximum possible speed safe for the Captain. The jump was risky. The doctors, Tony and Elyssa knew that. They had to try to save her if they could. The Prime Minister of England was with her mother in the medical bay. Because of problems with the British government if he just disappeared the Prime Minister was transported back to London before they jumped.

On the morning of the second day of the jump the ship came out of jump speed a matter of minutes from World One Sam. Danielle had returned to her duties and Staerr still had some repair work that had to be done before reactivation. Captain Davis had returned to the New Iberia and had complete confidence in Danielle's ablity as Captain. Rather than attempt a transport she opted to have the Captain's yacht take her to the surface. Before she arrived the staff on the planet had her house prepared for her. Her mother disembarked first and watched as her daughter was carried into her house. The amazing creatures that terified her before now by their very presence gave her comfort in this difficult time. Alina still unresponsive to any stimulus was laid in her bed surrounded by medics and doctors and equipment so advanced earthly medicine would never see their equal. The evening of her first day on Sam came and the darkness matched the feeling in her mother's heart. As the sun rose in the north Alina moved her hand to touch her mother's. The medics were very pleased that the planet was helping her. They did not understand how or why but it was undeniable bringing her here was the right thing to do.

An emergency flash message from World One Sam was sent to the Long Island, Lincoln and the New Iberia simultaneously. Steeling them selves for the worst outcome they connected the message to ship wide so all would hear at the same time they did. A raspy weak voice said, "I am holding you responsible if there is a scratch on my ship. You know that don't you?"

A New Beginning

THE FEELINGS IN the house compound was considerably more jovial than a few days before. It had been several days since Alina's mother had gone missing and no trace had been found in that time. This time there had not been any giants seen near her or any of those odd looking dogs. Her reappearance would be as surprising as her mother's change of emotions. No longer weeping uncontrollably she was again happy and smiling with a positive outlook. Her family felt sorry for her because she said she was with Alina and helped her get better. Alina's body was tumbling through the dark emptiness of space having been struck by the meteorite in the head killing her instantly. If that had not killed her the concusion of the exploding air pack on her back would have. The doctors recommendation of the Captain remaining here on World One was not met with resentment or any sense of disagreement. She grieved for those who gave their lives for her and regretted not being able to honor them in their last time.

A new Tretret commander stood near her and she would often reach for his arm to help her rise and walk. She had lost weight since her injury and was almost a feather in the Tretret's arm. As days passed the planet's effects helped her get stronger and stronger. A gift from Wendy arrived for Alina. Opening it there was a gallon of chocolate ice cream. The Prime Minister of England sent a message of happiness and relief that she was getting better. The sentiment was not reflected by the British crown. After more than eighteen days on World One Sam Alina transported aboard the Long Island in a wheel chair that didn't need wheels. Danielle was on the bridge as she always had been since returning to duty. Her power cells had been replaced with new ones and she was fully in command. Tony, Mike, the Tarnet Commander and many of the Captains she had served with welcomed her aboard her ship. The doctors still would not let her assume command again, not just yet until they were sure she was able to.

She asked Danielle to set course for the Lunar City cemetery. Alina felt it was her duty as the Captain and their friend to say goodbye to them personally. After a few days at maximum sub jump velocitiy earth sector was a few hours away. Alina was standing in her suit prepared to board the battlecraft to go to the moon's surface. The security team was ready having cleared any stones near the Captain away from her. Shields up and ready to deflect any errant stones that might find her a nice meal the Captain walked among the new graves. She wept openly at the grave of her former Tretret commander. The Strefdan graves were hard to see. They were like family to her and now she stood at the foot of their graves. The cemetery that seemed so small and unassuming now held the honored dead of the Planetary Council. Standing next to her was Alina's mother. Overwhelmed at being on the moon she was happy to be there because her daughter needed her. But she would be on a volcanic planet if that was where Alina needed her to be. The Prime Minister of England and his security maintained a respectful distance to give the Captain privacy.

Her family would shake their heads in disbelief when their mother talked about being on the moon with Alina and her ship's crew. Where she came up with this planet World One Sam was a mystery to them. But there was something different about her. She looked younger. Even her hair was different. The hair color was her normal color and the gray that was everywhere now there was little more than a few strands of gray here and there. Her eyesight was much better than before she disappeared. She no longer used glasses to read her books and magazines. They were skeptical at the very least when she mentioned the Prime Minister of England until she recieved cards and gifts from his office.

The Sherman police could not answer why she just turned up out of the blue in her own yard as if nothing had happened. There was a rose that none of the nursery companies had ever seen before in her yard and could not identify where it came from. An answer that it was called the 'Captain's Rose' meant nothing to them. There was a dog with her now and if the police did not know better the silly thing understood what they were saying to Mrs. Grant. An animal control officer tried to take it and the dog bit him. The man died from the bite in a few seconds. An autopsy revealed an extremely toxic venom in his blood with canine DNA mixed in. Obviously the sample in the lab was contaminated and was thrown out. Dogs are not venomous. The venom still does not have an anti toxin available.

Twenty nine days from her injury as she walked onto the bridge she was met with, "Captain on the bridge." Mike asked if she was ready to assume command again and she said yes she was. Placing her hand on the pedastel Captain Davis said that command was now transferred to her and that Captain Grant was going to begin a life altering adventure. She laughed and taking her chair she looked around at the bridge crew that was ready for her orders. Since Staerr was back as third in command the communications officer was Sandra once more. "Captain," she said, "message from the Illinois Lincoln priority grade one." "Connect message." "Next time you try to scare us you are on your own. Seriously Alina, you know all of us are and will always be there to watch your back. Captain Davis thinks of you as his little girl and me, well I see you as my family. A little sister so you need to obey your older brother." "That is not very likely. I didn't obey my brothers in Texas. Can't see any reason to change now." "That's what I figured you would say. I tried."

"Time for new beginnings Alina." Captain Davis told her. "The ship was refurbished during your vacation and is up to date. Changes in engines that reflect some of the discoveries on the Constellation have been implemented in your engines. Your weapons power is increased because they are channeled through your secondary engine's systems. By the way the planet of the trafficers? We found it and destroyed it. Couldn't save alot of their victims befroe they killed them but we got them. They won't be selling any world's peoples anymore. The attack on you and the ship was not entirely fault of the Orion but the Tarnet went to the new Orion world and turned it into ash. The other worlds involved in the attack are still being sorted out. It will take time to find them all."

Without thinking Alina reached behind her and her new Tretret commander's hand was there. During her time on Sam the vital importance of the Tretret and Strefden and all the others protecting her was made so very apparent. Their presence was comforting and their dedication to her was proven time and time again. The Medusan touched her shoulder and told her, "Welcome back Captain." William stood just in front and to her side where he always was. Danielle and Staerr were next to her on either side of her chair and Alina realized how much this meant to her. Her command, her ship and her crew. She could not fathom her life without all this around her. It was as much a part of her as breathing. She was not sure if the ship lived because of her or she lived because of the ship. The Captains she served with were her family as much and maybe more so than her family on earth.

Captain Davis said it was time for new beginnings. Maybe he was right it was indeed time to start anew. Facilities had been rebuilt on Terra Two so it too had a new beginning. Mystery eighteen thousand three hundred and six still remains unsolved. The sun above the new Orion world rose without the planet greeting it's rays. The Planetary Council's enemies withdrew when Orion was destroyed. The Grant's Constellation carries a civilization to an exo-moon that will support them for their own new beginning. Alina rose and walked around the bridge. She paused to take a deep breath happy she was able too.

The view screen showed a region of space the Long Island had not explored and the ship was fully operational and ready for her new mission. New beginnings, new missions, new worlds and new friends were yet to be discovered. And yes, unfortunately, new enemies would be found too.

THE END

New Day Rising

By Steven Lowe
(Writing as J.I. McKinney)

It has been a few weeks since my excursion into betrayal in Louisiana. I have had to watch my back ever since no matter what identity I take. There are forces at work here I cannot deal with. Powers high in governments around the world want me dead. It is no longer just the GRU. Killing the agent I was supposed to be traded for in China was a bad move. Killing the one who set me up for the trade was the end of my usefulness as an agent. Sam Daniel's is truly dead. All that is left is continuing new identities, continuing the lies and deceit that has become part of me and much to my regret continuing the hunter in me. I can't remember the last time I used my real name Sam Daniels. I have had so many names in the last few years I almost forgot it.

I thought my time in Camden, Maine was probably the nicest for me. The smell of the sea and the people were really comforting to me after all I have been through. Funny how a ratty seabag will get you real respect in a small town. Small things mean alot to some people and I had almost forgotten what that thinking means. People see what they want to see. An identity is what that thinking is all about. Whether it is a seaman, cowboy or a man that likes to stay to himself people see in someone else what they see in themselves. Would go back there but that would create a pattern that could be followed. The possibility of going overseas has presented itself recently. I found one of my buddies in the company that was released under cost cutting requirements. He was fired two years before he could retire with a decent pension so he has no love lost for those callous morons in Langely. He will supply me with passports, id's and backgrounds that will stand the scrutiny of the Russian Intelligence or any other digging into my past.

It is something to think about for sure. I have pretty much worn out my welcome in the United States. Albuquerque, New Mexico is an interesting city. The city government is a quandary of misunderstanding. The city itself has a lot of promises to explore. The Albuquerque, Santa Fe and Belen region has a combined population approaching two million citizens. Easy enough to disappear into with very little effort. Another city where a new face does not raise an eyebrow is perfect for me. My identity is a Hispanic one and I fit right into the city's majority peoples. I find the food will take a little time to get used to but once I have it is habit forming. Had an enchilada with jabanero Chile a few days ago and haven't had any colds or flu since. Going to Europe or eastern Europe has been a strong desire to me for some time. I speak several European languages courtesy of my time with the Company. They will serve me well when I do go. England is the doorway to Europe. If I do not choose to go to France by ship there is a tunnel under the English channel. I think the fresh air of the sea is preferable to a smog enshrouded tunnel despite the air purifying system.

I booked passage on one of the smaller cruise lines, changed my name again, got a different haircut and colored contacts made my eyes brown.

Drawing on one of the many languages I was taught during my tenure with the company I was able to pull off a decent French accent in my speech. I saw people whom I worked with before that had retired and discovered that living shipboard was better than living in a house surrounded by others so close you could flip a penny in their yard from your back door. When I walked by them they gave no indication they recognized me but then trained as an agent they wouldn't if they did. They could be a problem if they recognized me, time will tell. Shipboard accidents happen frequently. Less frequently a man overboard occurs during a cruise but it does happen. Lying out on the deck a waiter brought me a drink with a napkin under it. There was a note on the napkin. See him at seven tonight in the main dining salon for the crew. There was a coded message with it indicating I was being watched by another passenger on the fantail. White shorts and blue shirt with a redheaded woman next to him.

I walked to the fantail right next to the couple which he did not expect me to do. Trouble like this has to be handled directly and soon as possible. I acted like I was trying to stop an argument between them when he slipped under the fantail railing. His companion was a pawn. Someone he found that made him look good standing next to. I stifled a scream from her with a kiss and a needle that made her very unsteady as if she was drunk. By the time the crew and passenger manifest was checked it was a full day too late. His momentary companion couldn't remember anything from the day or evening before. I met the note man as planned in the crew dining area. I explained that the gentleman would not be completing the voyage and left it at that. He told me I had a knack for causing trouble. The FBI suspected I was still alive but my tracks were buried deep. He said he was sorry about my loss. Heard about the man hanging from the bridge. Terrible when those things happen absolutely tragic. Like me he had died many times on a mission. Once he was a farmer, then an office worker and the last I heard a technician at a computer repair shop. He was not a ghost. He had retired and stayed retired. Still got his pension every month as well as a paycheck from the cruise line. He was doing very well financially. It seemed that the cruise lines had drawn several former agents to their employ. Of course with pristine references and doctored resumes there was little doubt they would not be considered prime material for the cruise line.

Note man handed me an envelope with cash and a passport and French drivers license and walked away. A pistol was waiting for me in the locker at the train station number fourteen zero four. Inside I found the pistol, three clips, a small four inch push dagger and a stack of well wishes from people who remembered me. I was not alone. That feeling of being someone beside my identity was something I did not expect. Unlike in the U.S. here I had a network I could rely on. Retired agents that had followed my exploits in the United States. My methods were clean and I didn't leave clues behind. I moved around and the frequency of disappearances in locations I was supposed to be in fit my profile as they knew it when we were on missions. The GRU had approached them quietly wanting my location. They didn't know who they were talking about. Once retired you are out of the loop. Langely didn't like leaks and nosy retired employees sticking their nose where it didn't belong. French police were going aboard the cruise ship wanting to know about one of their men that was on the cruise with a redhaired woman as a companion. When they did not find him foul play was suspected in his disappearance. The tapes of that time period had been erased. Ten minutes of the fantail surveillance was missing.

Customs would not X-ray art because it ruins it. A visual inspection by hand would be done if there was a question. My donations from the cartel were in the crate of a painting with diplomatic pouch seal on it. I followed the truck delivering the painting to a safe house and filled two gym bags with my ill gotten proceeds from inside it. When I disembarked I watched the traffic patterns looking for the most common type of vehicles. I purchased a Citroen model about seven years old in serious need of paint and when I drove it would not be noticed. I remembered a route from many years before on a mission that didn't happen. My team and I were merely enjoying long overdue vacation time. In daytime the country side was much different and was actually beautiful to see. Still playing the tourist role I would pull over to the side of the road and point a camera at the scenery. I picked up a tail not far behind me and cursed myself for being sloppy. They would have to be dealt with but this was not the place for it. Getting back into the car I kept them in my mirrors so I could see them when they made their move. When they did make it I dropped a number of spikes in the road. I could see when they reached them because their car veered off the road down an embankment. It wouldn't kill them but the injuries would leave deep scars.

Now that I knew my cover was blown I would have to make some changes in my actions. Unlike in the U.S. here I had friends I could call on. By nightfall I had a new identity, weapons and a lady I had worked with before on a mission as my wife to give me additional cover story. In the morning her husband would know nothing about the evening before. She, as I found out, was not in a happy marriage anyway so drugging him gave her some sense of satisfaction. I mentioned in passing the herbs that Alexandra put in the Tsar's tea to make him more compliant with her wishes. Finding hensbane might be a problem but anything is possible when you have contacts in low places. I was warned that additional GRU agents were spotted on the streets of Nice. The bet was that I was the reason they were there. I refused to accept the bet. INTERPOL had become involved in the disappearance of the French police officer. Time to give them a pawn. London station had a few losers on file that would eagerly confess to a crime if they became notorious criminals. Killing a French police officer would make them hunted men and their pictures and names would be known Europe wide. Infamous murderers and innocent of the crime. The noteman obtained fake documents and photos showing them pushing the officer under the fantail rail. With the pictures, documents and their confessions INTERPOL would not be looking for me. A trial would be inconvenient so they had to have an accident in the prison yard to prevent one. With no additional evidence to the contrary the case was closed.

The INTERPOL investigators are not fools. This case reeked of CIA or another intelligence agency's involvement. They could not help but see people they knew were GRU, Chinese, Iranian, British or German intelligence in their fair cities it seemed overnight. Something was going to happen and it would be a major headache for them when it did. Leaves and days off were cancelled until this thing broke. The local governments were mystified by all this activity although a great deal of money was being spent in their towns as a result. My sources told me of the sudden influx of community peoples and by the eve of the third day I was in Patagonia far from the smouldering cauldron. Patagonia, Argentina is at the southern tip of South America. The town of Esquel in the Chubut Province, and my destination has a population of about thirty three thousand souls. When I arrived in early July it was a balmy thirty four degrees. Not your summer beach destination by any means but it provided the cover I needed to disappear for awhile. With a small population spotting someone that didn't fit was not difficult. Pity they didn't look closer at the old man at the restaurant as they passed. Some were within eighteen feet of the man they were looking for and walked right past me. That they were in Esquel at all spoke of the intense pressure the GRU was employing to find me. I would have to move on soon but I knew all roads and any way in or out was covered. On the Pacific side of Argentina, Esquel did have possible exit points. Either I was going to have to be very good at getting past the guards set up to find me or kill a few which would definitely tell them I was there. I didn't come to Esquel to die.

My best chance of survival was to make it to Buenas Aires and disappear into the cities population. A city as large as Buenas Aires would give me more than ample cover and time to recoup my lost invisibility to the GRU. I could never relax because I knew even here the Russians had eyes everywhere. Staying alive was becoming more of a challenge over here than I anticipated. Using store windows and car mirrors to check my six helped spot potential trouble before it got to me. For now I was OK. Throw away cell phones were my best bet for communication as they literally were thrown away if I thought i was being tracked with it. Again I purchased sterile clothing from different stores in different parts of the city always watching closely for anything or anyone that did not fit. An itch in my back told me that I was being watched. Usually when I felt this it meant I was being watched by a sniper. I moved into a store entrance next to me and using a clothing rack scanned the opposite buildings for any sign of them. The building directly opposite the store I was in, third floor window on the west end, was where he was. Idiot was another pawn. Christ I get tired of these stupid amateur want to be's. Half of the rifle barrel was actually outside the window pointing down toward me. I would normally walk away from something like this but decided to play a little game with her, as it turned out, instead.

Going out a rear door I came out in the alley along the wall of the building. Using an errant brick on the side as a rest I took aim at the shooter and tickled the trigger. The shot sounded like a muffled cough and I heard a woman's scream when it hit. It was not a fatal shot by intent. I meant to hurt the shooter not kill them. The shooter would not try this game again if she was smart, but by her being a pawn, that is not a hallmark of their character. At some point in time we might meet again and this time the shot would not be to wound. It would be hours before her handlers would check on her. The police radio said nothing of a potential sniper or someone being shot in her area. I had that much of a cushion to fade into the city streets and disappear. I knew the GRU would not give up in their quest to make me a ghost. No grave or tomb for me. No, I might be dropped with weights into the sea or my body parts might be found here and there. An unidentifiable burned mass might be located somewhere in another part of the country. As in Esquel I did not come to Buenas Aires to be unidentified remains in the city morgue.

In no small part due to the noteman on the cruise ship I had new passport, identification and credit line when I boarded the flight at five forty five in the evening. Eleven and a half hours later we landed in London Heathrow airport. On the flight there were two GRU no doubt as watchmen in case I was spotted. Their bodies arrived along with the rest of the passengers but never walked off. Everyone was detained and identifications and passports were checked and questioned. INTERPOL was on the report immediately. Their interrogation was child splay for me. I thought of playing with their heads but decided playing stupid was my best option. As I left the airport I saw FBI agents I had worked with before and kept walking without saying anything. With my alterations they did not recognize me which was advantageous for me and life saving for them. I had no feelings either way for the flap this would cause between the Russians and the British government. In reality I didn't exist on paper and in time my compatriots would erase me on the computers in Washington. Sam Daniels died years before therefore I didn't exist either. The convenience that created was comforting. Dead men can't be arrested for crimes committed when they are dead.

I chose a hotel near Kensington Palace, despite the tourist promotions, there is additional security because of the hotel's location. Can't have a tourist using the hotel to launch an attack against the Queen wouldn't be kosher activity. MI-5 and MI-6 both had covert stations near or in the hotel itself. GRU agents in the hotel would certainly draw their interest. INTERPOL already alerted to something in the air was working at speed to find out what and where. An incident in London near the Palace would create a stir they didn't want to deal with. I was in the hotel restaurant sitting next to a near side wall so I could see anyone coming in. The first thing most of those looking for me did was look along the back or far sides of the restaurant. That gave valuable seconds to see them first. She walked into the restaurant alone. She was so out of place it was ridiculously obvious who she was. A bandage on her right shoulder could have been from my bullet grazing her. Major mistake was her hand was buried in her purse the entire time like she was grasping something. This wench was a pawn for her controllers. So far the GRU had not spent a dollar on their pawns. I injured one, four in Cheyenne had run away and I had killed the rest.

I left walking right behind her marking her appearance for later target identification. An envelope was waiting for me at the front desk from the noteman. A new passport, cash and credit cards and a key to a bank safety box. I opened the bank safe box and found a package marked from an optical shop near by. The moment I picked it up I knew it was a gun. Walking out without opening the package I feigned reaching for my car keys and dropping them as GRU agents walked by across the street. My head was below a car door so they did not see me. I got a taxi and had him drive me to an address I remembered as a safe house. As we got closer I could see it was now a parking lot for a shopping mall. Time to go to plan B. I paid the driver and walked toward one of the store entrances keeping delivery trucks between me and the road behind me. The mall was crowded and gave me instant cover as soon as I walked a few feet inside. A Bobby came up to me and asked if I was an American. I handed him a passport from Germany and in my best German accent said no I was German. He switched to German and told me he knew me from years before with the agency. I was being watched closely by a woman in a red dress and cream colored top. He gave me back my passport, said thank you, sorry for the inconvenience and walked away.

I moved to a store entrance window behind a clothes rack, looked out into the chaos of the mall hallway and picked up the wench almost immediately. My first shot grazed her shoulder. The next one would close her eyes permanently. She walked by the store looking for me and in a few minutes I heard screams from down the way. She lay in a growing pool of blood gasping for breath. Her neck was sliced open and she died unseeing right at me. The GRU had killed her because she failed in her assignment twice in a row. No matter where I go people die. By my hand or by someone else's people still die. Noteman was right beside me and said we had to go before the police arrived. A car was waiting for me in the lot. It was small, economical and as common as the rain in England. Old, in need of a paint job and some light body work it was invisible on the streets or highway. It was the perfect transportation for me.

I had a plan that required a little help from my friends. A bomb made by a man no longer among the living was waiting for me in a box not far from the hotel. Time to speed things up and have the hidden come into the light. A note lying on the seat of a police car said there was a bomb in the lobby of a hotel near the palace. It didn't specify which one but was close to Hyde Park. A major incident alert was initiated and INTERPOL, as expected, was in the forefront of the responders. So were the GRU agents hiding among the hotel guests. Trying to blend in a little too hard they attracted the INTERPOL agent's attention. Ear whigs was a clue they weren't tourists hoping to see the Queen from a distance. Watching from a second story window I have to admit they were quick to isolate them. TV cameras got the rest of the commotion. Their covers blown they tried to run and disappear. London's best were close on their heels and escape was not possible. Moscow would have them out of jail in an hour but they were no longer useful. It happens to the best of agents.

The bomb was located by the Met's bomb dogs and disarmed. It's similarities to other bombs like it from a man known to be dead sent INTERPOL looking into a copy cat bomber. Confusion is a great way to lose yourself in someone else's despair. I was watching the spectacle with great satisfaction and saw among those detained by the Met two men I knew well. Alexi Orsokov and Vladamir Yorovsky were two of the GRU's best problem eliminators. Never photographed or positively identified by any government until today. I will send flowers to Scotland Yard with a sympathy card that says Kiss My Ass before Moscow gets them released. Noteman delivered the flowers and left them there with the officer at the front saying they were sent by an anonymous individual. That will, if nothing else, tell them who blew their whole operation. To have them in London means I am very close to the top of the GRU's most wanted list. These two only come out to kill those considered most dangerous to Moscow. I like England but it is time to go somewhere else. INTERPOL agents, during an interrogation of both of them, delivered the flowers to them and wanted to know who sent them and why. A representative of the Russian Consulate came in at that point and left Scotland Yard with them walking behind her.

It wasn't a complete loss for INTERPOL. They were identified, photographed, voice and finger printed and water glasses they used provided their DNA.

Rio de Janeiro is a huge city. One of the most visited cities in the Southern Hemisphere means new faces are invisible on the streets. The weather is wonderful and some of the most gorgeous women in the world. Got to keep my priorities straight. Survival first then the women of Brazil. A wise man was asked what was the greatest skill a man could have and he kept silent. I was in one of the many small shops on the beach sitting so I could observe, and not be seen myself, without anyone getting behind me in the process. Can't say anything about the waters on the beach but the beach itself is covered with distractions. Have to keep my mind on the here and now. Was looking at the traffic out on the street and several cars pulled up to the curb. These men were dressed wrong and acted wrong for the location. Behind the window the sun's glare hid me from their view but I saw them quite clearly. They began to divide into teams going into individual stores. These were wet assets no doubt about that. They were hired killers.

Not even a day in Brazil and the GRU was here hunting me. Someone was telling them where I was going and where I would possibly be. I had a mole in my friends. A leak I would have to find and terminate with extreme prejudice. I was sure it wasn't the noteman. It was just a feeling I had he would not betray me. The others I did not know as well and could have been any of them. Trust is one of the strongest most valuable assets an agent has until it is broken. Someone shattered the trust I had for them. The noteman was close and took out one of the assets. The second never lived long enough to warn the others. Someone always dies when I am around. I accepted that many years ago. I thought my killing days were over when I retired from the Company. I guess I was wrong. The woman that was my wife in Paris was there and she took out another of them with a needle to his heart. When we met again she said she had not had so much fun in years. Her husband, it seems, was caught with another man's wife and died in her bed. "Oh well," she said," things happen."

I thought it ironic that I was alone, without any support of any kind in the U.S., but had friends here that the agency trained and probably set up in apartments or houses and then wrote off because they are retired. Reaching maximum retirement age or just no longer useful to them they were buried in a file no one looked at. I told them of the suspected leak and didn't know where to start looking for the traitor. Trish had an idea of who it might be and for me to let her do her thing. Her thing was interrogation with the agency.

Noteman and I settled into waiting for the others in the team to find their compatriots and then join them. The Rio de Janeiro police really were not going to like us. Even if they would never know who we were. We made it more difficult to find them by taking them to the slums and opening their wallets. The headlines in the English print newspaper the next morning was filled with a story of several European men, suspected of having ties to the drug trade, were found dead in the slums. Their money and valuables were missing. Surprise, surprise. With the back log of thousands of unknowns already, identifying their remains would be put on the back burner and the bodies in a locker with the rest of the city's unidentified dead.

Trish was correct about the mole. Sad thing when people commit suicide. The leak sealed I could move around more freely and openly, so to speak, than before. The GRU was becoming obsessed with me. There were two choices. Kill me, their preferred choice or put me on a do later list. Putting a bounty on my head was an option but then there would be hundreds of claims for the money. Besides if one person talked to the wrong person the media onslaught would be killing to the whole operation. Keep it in tight and wait. I did the tourist thing in Rio as visitors are expected to do and then moved on.

Copenhagen, Denmark is as far from Rio in natures as any two cities can be. With a population approaching five hundred eighty four thousand it is a bustling modern city. The size and popularity as a travel destination makes disappearing into its streets easy. When I checked into my hotel there was another envelope waiting for me from the noteman. A passport from Denmark, travel itinerary, credit cards and a box was delivered to my room. Noteman didn't send the box. I had been very careful to cover my tracks from Rio. The GRU could not know I was here. Trish called and said she sent me a box of special cupcakes from Ireland. They had medicinal doses of the best rye Scotches and Whiskeys available in the Emerald Isles. A thank you for making her feel useful again. She did the grieving wife thing at her husband's funeral and when out of sight in a funeral service limo opened a small bottle of American bourbon and downed it in one drink.

She told me the next day she had not enjoyed a night's sleep so well in a long time. A white print skirt and short sleeve blouse she was all smiles when she went shopping in Vienna the day after that. Austria in the summer. Nothing like it.

I wanted to send a message to the GRU they could not ignore and remembering I had someone on ice I decided to make it obvious I was still very much alive. With help from my friends over here my plan made international news. Mid August in Phoenix, Arizona usually has daytime temperatures over one hundred seven degrees. From South Mountain Park, the largest municipal park in the United States, Phoenix police received a 911 call they thought was a joke but had to check it out anyway. Who they found was the GRU station agent from Washington, D.C., missing for three months frozen solid. The chatter between Moscow, Phoenix police, the NSA and the FBI was not cordial.

International news agencies picked up on the story from Phoenix news reports and the city became the place to be. The first question was what did the CIA have to do with this? This was a political assassination the CIA's forte. Denial was met with calls of outrage at being lied to in a public interview. The cover story was released the GRU killed their own station agent for undisclosed reasons. If the GRU killed their own agent why was he frozen and left in a public place to be found by anyone? Hours later the story was changed again. The U.S. State Department took the brunt of the backlash on the incident. I didn't care because in Switzerland the evening was pleasant and my company was gorgeous. The noteman and my wife in Paris walked up next to me and he said, "You know you are truly demented. I like the way you think. I yield to the master of deviousness." I said, "I knew I liked you for some reason. You are humble." The three of us were laughing and almost missed the woman approaching from the right with her left hand hidden.

Trish saw her first and stopped her in her tracks. A brief struggle and our visitor went over the balcony into a chasm without a sound as she fell hundreds of feet into the rocks below. Dinner was waiting inside and we thought no more of her. The finding of a woman's body in the rocks below a restaurant on the mountainside above was on the news the next day. With the remains damaged as they were it would take time to identify her. She was identified after some time. An agent of Iranian intelligence her presence in Switzerland, denied by Iranian leaders, was under question. Her presence was a glaring sign that the GRU knew or suspected I was here. Time to move on again.

CPSIA information can be obtained
at www.ICGtesting.com
Printed in the USA
BVHW030152170520
579803BV00006B/36/J